To Maddy,
Thinking of you—
enjoy the read.

Lynn M

I had been taught that the language of friendship was founded in meaning, but sometimes words were hard to ignore—especially if they spelled murder...

There was a torn note tucked under my windshield wiper. Odd. I unfolded the plain white paper. An involuntary cry of fear escaped my lips as I read it. I looked up and saw Jo, Mary, and Erica rushing to my side.

"Izzy!" Jo shouted, running over.

"What is it? What's wrong?" Mary cried, she and Erica not far behind.

I was certain they could see the fright in my eyes.

I handed Mary the scribbled, torn note, and she, Jo, and Erica huddled together to read it.

You will die next if you don't stop meddling.

Mary turned white and looked terrified. Jo grabbed my hand and looked around frantically.

Erica looked shocked but put a firm hand on my shoulder in an effort to soothe my nerves. "You're okay, Isabelle. Someone is just trying to scare you." She held my gaze. "Take a deep breath."

I followed Erica's instructions and reread the note. Something about it wasn't making sense to me, but I couldn't quite put my finger on what it was.

The first book in the new Izzy Walsh Mystery Series!

An oceanfront estate in the beautiful New England town of Twin Oaks is the ideal setting for Isabelle Walsh and her close-knit group of friends to celebrate their annual girls' weekend in 1953.

While off to a promising start, the weekend quickly goes awry as murder interrupts the fun and the hostess is accused of the shocking crime. Izzy quickly realizes it is up to her to save her innocent friend and bring the murderer to light.

Keen intuition and quick wit are Izzy's only tools. She must use them to find the dark truth before the killer brings her investigation to a dead stop…

KUDOS for *The Girls' Weekend Murder*

"In Izzy Walsh, McPherson has created a character who's fun, witty, and loyal to a fault, with a fierce determination to prove her friend is innocent of murder—the perfect combination for an amateur sleuth. Told with a unique and refreshing voice, this is one you will want to keep on your shelf to read again whenever you're feeling nostalgic. A really fun read!" ~ Pepper O'Neal, author of the award-winning *Black Ops Chronicles* series

In *The Girls' Weekend Murder* by Lynn McPherson, Izzy Walsh joins a group of friends at one's seaside home for an annual girls' weekend, where they eat, laugh, gossip, catch up on each other's lives, and generally have fun. That is, until the hostess's husband is murdered and his wife is arrested for the crime. Being a true and loyal friend, and never having a single doubt that her friend is innocent, Izzy pulls out all the stops to clear her friend's name, as she doesn't think the police will do a good enough job since they are convinced his wife killed him. But Izzy knows better. However, as determined as she is to expose the truth, someone else is just as determined to keep it hidden. Set in 1953 New England, the story takes you back to a simpler place and time, where life was much less confusing and, while murder was taken just as seriously, interfering in a police investigation usually didn't land you in jail. If you like historical mysteries, that you can't figure out until the end you're going to love this one. ~ *Taylor Jones, The Review Team of Taylor Jones & Regan Murphy*

The Girls' Weekend Murder by Lynn McPherson is the story of friendship, love, and betrayal. When our heroine, Izzy Walsh, and her two friends, Jo and Ava, travel to a third friend, Mary's, home for an annual weekend get-together, they are expecting good food, cold drinks, fun, laughter, sunshine, and female bonding. What they are not expecting is for Mary's husband Charles to die suddenly or for Mary to be arrested for his murder. Furious at the police detective's lack of insight—since he can't immediately see that her friend is innocent—Izzy vows to solve the crime herself. With the help of her two other friends, Jo and Ava, Izzy embarks on a quest to find the killer. But what she discovers is a lot more questions and, even worse, what clues they do manage to gather point to Mary as the most likely suspect. Not at all what Izzy hoped to accomplish. McPherson's character development is superb. I adored Izzy who, for a woman in 1953, is both a spitfire ahead of her time and utterly charming. If you want a heartwarming mystery that will keep you guessing until the very end, you can't miss with *The Girls' Weekend Murder*. ~ *Regan Murphy, The Review Team of Taylor Jones & Regan Murphy*

ACKNOWLEDGMENTS

This book cannot begin without first thanking a few kindred spirits who helped me fulfill my dream: Kerrin Hands, Jen Bistolas, Jamie Milligan, Averyl McPherson, and Dad. Thank you.

I am also grateful to my Aunt Stella and my mom, Rita, who read each and every word of this book in order to sort through some unusual sentence arrangements and bizarre word uses.

The team at Black Opal Books: I am filled with gratitude for your hard work and efforts. You took a chance on me and taught me more than I knew I needed to know!

Mr. Brian Switzer, the most phenomenal English teacher, who first ignited my love of reading with an introduction to Jane Austen, Emily Bronte, and William Makepeace Thackeray. I will always remember your lessons, your influence, and your wit. Gratias tibi ago.

Finally, I must thank Troy Cusolle, my soul mate, who has supported and encouraged me in every way. I love you.

The

Girls' Weekend

Murder

AN IZZY WALSH MYSTERY

Lynn McPherson

A Black Opal Books Publication

THE GIRLS' WEEKEND MURDER ~ An Izzy Walsh Mystery
Copyright © 2017 by Lynn McPherson
Cover Design by Kerrin Hands
All cover art copyright © 2017
All Rights Reserved
Print ISBN: 978-1-626946-45-3

First Publication: APRIL 2017

Published by Black Opal Books **http://www.blackopalbooks.com**

DEDICATION

For Scarlett and Remy.
You are my light, my laughter, and my love.

Chapter 1

It was the summer of 1953, and I was feeling good. In fact, I was feeling great. Getting all dolled up was a treat I rarely got to experience these days. This morning my husband and children refrained from knocking on the bathroom door for a full half hour in exchange for a pancake breakfast usually reserved for birthdays. That provided me with just enough time to get ready. I put on my favorite corset with a full blue skirt and crisp, white blouse. Then I applied matching indigo eyeshadow. Finally, I tackled my limp, straight hair. This would take a little extra effort. I carefully took the pin curlers out and tried to arrange it just like the picture I had in front of me from *Enchanted* magazine. I unleashed half a can of Aqua Net over it and neatly tucked a violet pansy behind my

ear to match my eyes. I took a final peek in the mirror
and was pleasantly surprised. I was ready to go cruising
on the open road. That's how I felt, anyways. More accurately, I would be driving responsibly through the subur-
ban town of Twin Oaks. But it was en route to a weekend
I had looked forward to all year.

It had been a long time since I'd been out on my
own. Every time I went out solo, I told myself I must do
it more often. But it didn't happen. My husband, Frank,
was extra sweet today by surprising me with the keys to
his fixed-up convertible. A bonus of having a mechanic
for a husband, I supposed. I had this grin on my face so
wide I looked like I was trying to sell toothpaste. *Okay, I
need to rein this in.* My excitement would land me in bed,
sleeping, by nine o'clock if I kept it up. But I couldn't
help it. Our girls' weekends had been reduced to a once-
a-year event, and I was giddy with anticipation. I still saw
the girls regularly but it was usually for a quick coffee or
playtime with our children. There simply wasn't time to
unwind and pal around. This was important to me because I needed to remember who I was other than the
roles I had in life, such as wife and mother. These were
my greatest joys, but I still delighted in occasionally re-
viving the immature young woman who loved silly antics
and laughing until her face hurt. I could hear her calling
to come out as I turned onto Ava's street.

Ava Russell, my best friend, could make anyone
laugh. Her amusing observations and sarcastic tone made

her hard to ignore. But it was her big heart that solidified my affection for her. She was a loyal, caring friend, in addition to—or maybe in spite of—her biting wit. I pulled into her driveway and turned off the car. No sooner had I done this than Ava's front door swung open and she was waving madly at me, making her gorgeous brunette locks bounce up and down on her shoulders. I could see a brilliant yet fiendish smile on her face highlighted by her signature red lipstick, which she swore never to leave home without.

"Izzy, what did you have to do to get Frank to let you take this beauty for the whole weekend? Or is it better I don't ask?"

She winked at me and I rolled my eyes.

"Ava, I believe proper etiquette is to start with a simple greeting, such as good afternoon, before giving me a hard time," I remarked.

"Oh, darling, you know I'm just jealous. Frank is such a prince. Bruce barely lets me use our car to go get groceries. If I didn't promise to bring him back some of those damn potato chips every time I went, I think it would be a real battle."

I laughed. "Bruce is a sweetheart. You make him sound like a brute."

"Izzy, please. I didn't say I'd lose the battle. He's just not as generous with his precious car. Never mind if he had a car like this!"

"I like to think Frank is simply that sweet but, in

truth, I think in the back of his mind he reassures himself that if anything happens to the car, he can easily fix it in the shop," I admitted.

Frank opened a mechanic shop following his return from the war. I would have said he loved cars, but that wasn't quite accurate. In fact, he loved engines. He was a hands-on problem solver and enjoyed figuring out how any engine worked and making it run smoothly. During the war, Frank joined the air force and became a proficient airplane mechanic. Since he joined as a skilled car mechanic to begin with, he mastered the craft and then taught it to others. Frank trained recruits on the Avro Anson airplane. Later in the war, upon his request, he went overseas to serve. That was a dark time for me, one I didn't like to think of often.

Chapter 2

We put Ava's bags in the trunk and headed out. As we drove away from Ava's home, the wind made her crinoline-lined floral skirt float up revealing a scandalous look at her long lean legs. I wasn't even sure if Ava was wearing stockings.

She let out a loud and joyous holler, "Izzy, I have been looking forward to this weekend for months."

"Me too," I declared, pushing away a sea of flowers from her encroaching skirt, "I wish we could do it more often."

"Izzy." Ava composed her outfit and gave me a stern look. "We are not the irresponsible young women we once were. We have children who would miss us and besides, I have to leave such detailed instructions on how to survive one weekend without me, I mean honestly, it takes weeks of planning—" She broke off in a giggle. "—I'll admit that I do add in a few extra chores I wouldn't normally bother with myself, just to make sure Bruce and the kids appreciate all the hard work I do."

I shook my head. "You have a terrible yet brilliant mind."

We drove through town and I suddenly felt nostalgic. I glanced over at Ava and felt thankful she was such a big part of my life.

She looked back at me, "Are they too much?"

"What?"

She lifted her polka dot kitten-framed sunglasses off her face and squinted. I could barely see her warm brown eyes behind the thick mascara, "The glasses—are they over-the-top?"

"They suit you perfectly," I answered, not trying to hide a smirk.

She had much more of an adventurous style than I did, as I rarely strayed from my plethora of pleated skirts and plain blouses.

She placed her sunglasses back over her eyes then glared at me through the dark lenses., "You know, the sarcastic tone you repeatedly berate me with will probably affect my self-confidence long-term, if it hasn't already."

I glanced at her and repressed a laugh. Ava had the kind of looks that could take a little bit of friendly teasing. I turned on the radio and was happy to hear Tony Bennett singing "Rags To Riches." It was one of my favorite songs.

"Do you ever think about how lucky we are to be from such a lovely place?" I thought out loud.

"Twin Oaks has everything one could want. It oozes charm and beauty, just like us," she quipped, forgetting her previous statement.

I persisted. "With the car factory opening, I worry it's going to change. There's housing going up everywhere."

"Izzy, when we were teenagers you used to criticize it for being too small and provincial. Remember when we wanted to run away to New York City?"

"I sure do, but now there's nowhere else I'd rather live. Although," I added, "I'd still love to run away to New York, but maybe for a long weekend instead."

"Sounds tempting, although New York may lose its allure once I see Paris. Bruce has finally promised me we will go next summer, as long as I curtail my spending a little. I'm going to hold him to it, too," Ava said defiantly.

"Have you told him Frank and I may be joining you?" I asked.

"No, but I'm sure he won't be surprised. Besides, he and Frank get along famously. He'll love it. Paris will be so fabulous, it would be a shame not to see it together. That is one adventure I'm already looking forward to."

It certainly wouldn't be our first. Ever since I met Ava in high school, we specialized in trouble. Never content to let the world pass us by, we were always looking for new challenges. It was how we came to meet our two closest friends, Jo and Mary.

It felt like it was just last week that we were standing in line for our first shift at the munitions factory. It was our way of contributing to the war effort. There was a simple ad in the newspaper asking women to join the fight and help win the war. Plus, having a feeling of personal freedom in our own life became important to us when we had no sense or control over what was happening in the rest of the world.

"Do you remember the first time we saw Mary? She looked so polished and sophisticated, even in that uniform. How did she do it?" I wondered.

"That's just Mary. She has a way of carrying herself that has an air of confidence," Ava asserted.

"Don't forget she was also our first boss," I reminded her.

"That's true. Demonstrating how to make weapons, in itself, gives a sense of marvel," Ava noted.

"Kinda weird that our first job was making guns, isn't it?" I pondered.

"Out of context, yes. But what isn't weird during wartime?"

"True," I agreed, "I have no doubt that small blessing of independence helped me remain sane. I always assumed that's why Mary was there, too."

"Well, it certainly wasn't the money. When you have as much money as she does, you don't do anything you don't want to," Ava reckoned.

"Maybe her regular club activities just didn't seem worthwhile during the war," I supposed.

"Wasn't it also around the same time Charles was opening his firm? I'm sure I remember her talking about him working really long hours."

"Maybe," I said, unconvinced, "It just seems a little crazy to live away from your husband *and* your ocean-front home."

Ava scoffed. "I'm surprised you never out right asked Mary what her reasons were for working and living with the rest of us."

"Well, actually I did," I admitted, "And she said exactly what you guessed: that Charles was busy and she felt more useful being at the factory and the dorm. It's a perfectly reasonable explanation."

"But you didn't buy it," Ava figured.

"It's not that I didn't believe her, it's just that I felt like she was holding back from telling me the *whole* truth. But Mary was like a den mother to us. She probably didn't want to burden us with her own problems."

"Or the simple and straightforward explanation she gave you *was* the whole truth but your inventive and inquiring mind wanted something juicier," Ava suggested.

"You make me sound perfectly ridiculous. A curious mind is a healthy mind," I said defensively.

"That may be true but I think what you're really wondering is whether it was something a little more personal that kept her away from home.".

"Okay, you got me. I've never felt all that comfortable with Charles. He just seems too good to be true," I admitted.

"Is it his nice suits or his winning smile?" Ava asked with an impertinent grin.

A deep flush filled my cheeks. "He comes across as charming and sophisticated, yes, but there's something about him I never trusted."

"You just can't quite put your finger on it," she said, continuing to mock me.

"That's right. Go with your gut," I quipped, holding my head up in an attempt to combat her ridiculing.

"After years of mistrusting him, did you ever consider maybe you're just overthinking it?" she postulated.

"It's possible," I grumbled.

"Well, you know what I think? You're just not used to talking to men who have his charisma or charm. It's your way of excusing our guys for not possessing such sophistication. You don't trust it because you've only seen it in the movies."

"You know how truly insulting that is to our husbands, right?" I said, wondering if—just maybe—she had a point.

"The only time I've seen Bruce in a tuxedo, he waddled around pretending to be a penguin. When I asked him to cut it out, his response was to quack. Do you see what I'm saying?" Ava said dryly.

"Do penguins quack? I don't think I've ever heard a penguin make a sound," I mused.

"That was on our wedding day," she added.

"You should be grateful you ended up with a guy who doesn't take himself too seriously. How many brooders did you date before you realized they weren't all that fun?" I reminded her.

She giggled. "What can I say? I was a sucker for a rebel."

"Yes, until you got tired of the moody moping," I recalled.

"I will admit that the dark, mysterious types are better in movies. It gets pretty annoying," she confessed.

"And how can you be the center of attention if your man is so self-involved?" I teased.

"Okay, you made your point. Bruce is pretty good at making me laugh—and I will grudgingly admit he's fairly thoughtful. But don't tell him I said so. He might get lazy," Ava warned.

"He's a hard working accountant. I'd call him anything but lazy. If he wasn't so bright, I'd ask if he was a little dim witted the way he spoils you. It's perfectly embarrassing."

"Oh, be quiet. He does his best, as he should, and that's all." She gave me a little nudge and we drove the rest of the way lost in our thoughts.

Chapter 3

W e didn't have far to go. We were picking Jo up from the bus station, just a few minutes down the road. She insisted on taking the bus part way, even though I was more than happy to go get her at her apartment. We parked the car, but left the radio on, and we hummed along to Patti Page's new hit, "(How Much Is) That Doggie in the Window." It was nice soaking up the sun's rays. I put my head back and closed my eyes. Memories from the war slowly drifted back, the endless days and nights in the factory. I tried to recall when we first met Jo. My mind drew a blank.

"Stop concentrating so hard, it'll give you wrinkles," Ava advised.

"How did we meet Jo? Did Mary introduce us?"

"It was wartime—" Ava began.

"Hey, just because I don't have your unusually ele-phant-like memory, there's no need to be condescend-ing," I interrupted.

She shot me a look of annoyance and continued. "I remember it vividly. It was 1943 and you and I had been at the factory for quite some time, over a year, I think. We were with Mary on a Friday night, trying to find a fourth player for our bowling team."

"Oh yes, that's right. Mary was trying to get us more involved in social activities and less involved in Friday night cocktails," I recalled.

"You got it. By then, the three of us had corrupted each other with excessive booze and card games. She was trying to expand our interests. In vain, of course," Ava noted.

"I think our enthusiasm for bowling would've only lasted a few weeks if you hadn't turned it into our memo-rable ritual of B and B," I reluctantly admitted.

Ava laughed. "Ha, yes, beer and bowling. So much for Mary's attempt to steer us away from the drinks."

"Jo fit into our team seamlessly. She had a killer spin, too. I don't think any of us could beat her strike count."

The rusty memories now came flooding back. Jo was from a farm where she lived with her parents and three brothers. Her oldest brother, Arnold, was her best friend. The other two brothers didn't show much interest in their petite, quiet sister. Arnold enlisted in the army against his parents' wishes and was killed in battle not long after. Jo felt the best way to honor Arnold's sacrifice and contribution to the war was to sign up at the factory. It was a sharp contrast to her parent's way of dealing with their son's death. They shut the world out further and stopped talking about him. Jo was then disowned. Mary helped ease her lonely transition from farm to factory life, and she slowly came out of her shell.

A grin crept up on my face as a comical memory replayed in my mind. "Do you remember what created your immediate attachment to Jo?"

Ava smiled, feigning modesty. "Of course, sweet thing. She thought I was a dead ringer for the great Jane Russell."

"Yes, and she was convinced you must be related somehow because you share a surname," I said.

"Until you ruined all the fun by informing her that I was a Russell only through marriage, you killjoy. You know, she is not the first person who has made the comparison," Ava informed me.

"As you remind me regularly, how could I? Besides, isn't that the reason you first dated Bruce? You thought it would be fun to daydream about donning your favorite actress's name. Low and behold, you actually fell for the quiet math whiz," I said.

"That's in the vault," she warned me, "Sometimes I remind myself we will have to be friends forever simply because you know too many of my secrets."

"Luckily, we have Mary and Jo to ease the pain," I concurred, "It didn't take long before the four of us were inseparable, did it?"

"Hard to resist the wisecracks and inventive spirits," Ava proclaimed.

"When the alternative is lonely and alone, yes, I think we had that beat," I lamented. "Have you actually talked to Jo lately?"

Ava scrunched up her nose, "No, I feel terrible but it's probably been at least a month. I hope she's doing okay."

"My money says she's doing just fine. It's been over a year since she left that toxic husband of hers."

"I still can't believe she stayed with that monster, Kevin, so long," Ava growled, "Eight years being knocked around? I'm as wary of divorce as the next gal, but there's certain situations where you just have to walk away, if not *run* away."

Jo returned to the farm after the war, hoping to reconcile with her family. Unfortunately, it was like stepping right back into the pain and grief she felt when she first left.

"No doubt it was loneliness that threw her into the arms of the first man she met," I reasoned.

"I know why she jumped *into* marriage so quickly, but why stay so long once the abuse started? All she had to do was call us. We would've been there immediately, and we wouldn't have judged her," Ava insisted.

"I think it took her that long to decide it wasn't her fault," I concluded.

Violence started about a year into Jo's marriage. Kevin had fought overseas and was grappling with combat exhaustion—a modern term for shell shock. It started out very infrequently but over the years became more routine, once Kevin gave up trying to deal with his emotional scars in any way but through the abuse of alcohol. Jo wanted desperately to help but it got to a point she feared for her safety. She confided in her mother. Instead of trying to help, her mother told Jo to go home and stop doing things to trigger his anger—just be a better wife. When that approach didn't work, Jo called Mary in desperation. Mary and Charles took her in. Jo lived with them for over a year while she attended secretarial school.

"I'm thrilled she got a fresh start. Poor thing deserved a break," Ava sympathized.

I let out a loud breath. "I can't wait to see her."

"Me too! What time is the bus supposed to get here?"

"Two-fifteen I think. It's ten-past-two now, you won't have to be patient much longer," I teased.

"You know, Izzy, I have become much more patient since we were kids. I have no problem sitting back and simply enjoying the sunshine while we wait." It was about two minutes later when Ava barked, "C'mon, ya damn bus, what's the hold up?"

I said nothing but chuckled to myself. I got out of the car and sat on the hood. It was hot but the humidity hadn't hit us yet. I hoped it wouldn't since I'd spent so long on my hair today. There was enough hair spray in it to freeze a bird flying overhead. I glanced in the mirror confidently. Aqua Net had, unfortunately, met its match. The convertible car had converted my hair from pinup to blowup, and all that was left of the pansy was a sticky, gross ball of purple glue hanging off my ear. I peeled it off and flicked it at Ava. She didn't notice.

"Were you going mention to me that my hair resembled a bird's nest?" I demanded.

"Oh, Izzy, it looks fabulous," she said dismissively with barely a glance over. "Your hair is raven-black and gorgeous. It simply looks like you're ready for some fun!"

"Or maybe that I've just had *too* much fun?" I countered.

"Don't be silly. I saw a photograph of Elizabeth Taylor on the beach, and it looked just like yours—windswept."

I felt mildly annoyed. "Did you sneak open that bottle of wine on our drive over here?"

"No, but I do have a treat," she said, digging through her purse. She pulled out a bottle of baby oil and started rubbing it on her arms. "May as well get a little color while we're waiting."

I reached behind the front seat of the car and grabbed my own bottle. "Never leave home without it."

"Great minds think alike," she declared.

"Or fools rarely differ," I proposed.

"Oh, stop arguing and get my back."

We had just a few minutes to soak up some sun when the bus came into sight around the corner. Ava and I jumped up and waited for Jo to exit the bus. As she did, I hit Ava on the arm.

"Oh, my goodness," I gasped.

Ava looked at me with a big smile, "Our little Jo is all grown up."

Jo had a sophisticated suit on, worthy of any fashion magazine. She was wearing a fitted blue jacket and a pencil skirt, hitting just below her knees. It was tailored so her usual petite, almost boy-like frame looked curvy and feminine. Her golden hair was short and curly, tucked under a black, trendy lampshade hat, looking ultra-modern. And most notably, she was wearing a smile that reached all the way up to her big brown eyes. It was quite the transformation, even from just a few months ago.

Ava and I rushed up to give her a big hug.

"Jo it is *so* good to see you. We've missed you!" I exclaimed.

"I've missed you too! I was so excited about today I couldn't sleep last night. I think I counted 1000 sheep before giving up and making some tea," she admitted.

Ava stood back to get a better look. "Well, Miss Jo, if this is what happens to you being away from us for just a few short months, maybe we should make it a year next time. You look simply gorgeous," she gushed.

Jo curtseyed and let out a giggle, "Thank you."

I was in full agreement. "Seriously, you look like you should be gracing the pages of *Modern Woman*."

"I'd have to thank Mary for that. It would take me six months to save up for an outfit like this. I love my new job, but office assistant isn't exactly the path to become wealthy. Mary had a bunch of clothes made for me as a sort of congratulations for my new start."

Ava wagged her finger at Jo. "It's not your new job, it's your new career."

I nodded my head in agreement. "Ava's right. Besides, Mary may have helped you look the part but it's your hard work that got you your new start."

"Thank you, girls." Then Jo added in a hushed tone so no one else could hear, "This may sound a little silly but seeing my reflection in the mirror on the way into work really helped me out. I almost felt like I was in a play and had a costume on."

Ava put her arm around Jo's shoulders. "Those mean brothers of yours would be eating their words right now if they could see you. There's not a trace of the fragile girl they used to call a runt."

Jo's eyes grew large. "Oh, she's in there all right, but I'm trying to calm her nerves in an effort to fit in with the office folks now."

Ava looked at Jo thoughtfully. "It's working."

"Independence agrees with you," I concurred.

Jo's big smile returned. "It's really different. But I love it," she admitted. "There's so much going on in town and at the newspaper!"

Ava subtly shook her hips. "It's fun to be around the hustle and bustle. I know I couldn't live the country life. It seems so isolated."

"That's true for us. But for people back home it's not isolated; It's not even lonely—it's simply quiet and peaceful," Jo explained.

I picked up Jo's small weekend bag. "I guess it just depends on your perspective—"

"Speaking of perspective," Ava interrupted. "It's almost three on this lovely Friday afternoon. Some people might see that as time to break for coffee. But with you girls by my side, I clearly recognize it as high time for a drink!"

Chapter 4

We hopped into the car and drove through town. There was a feeling of refined luxury in Twin Oaks that never got old. Mary's street was a prime example. It was lined with big, old trees and Victorian homes paired with manicured lawns and magnificent views. We drove slowly and took in the sprawling oceanfront estates overlooking the Atlantic.

Jo sighed audibly as we approached Mary's property. "I don't think I could ever grow tired of living here."

Ava lifted her sunglasses to take in a better look. "It takes me no time at all to adjust to life around these parts. After my last weekend at Mary's, I could hardly bring myself to go back to my regular chores. It felt positively indecent."

I chuckled silently to myself. I knew what she meant. We reached a long winding driveway and it led us to Mary's front door. We parked in front of the classic Victorian-style limestone home, surrounded by lush green gardens filled with big hosta plants and stunning hydrangeas.

Ava and Jo began to fix their tousled hair in the mirror of the car. I just hopped out without looking. I had given up and I knew it was better not to look at this point. Instead, I wandered down the footpath from the driveway to the edge of the cliff. There was a rocky ledge several feet above the ocean. The waves gently broke over the shore below and a gentle breeze was coming off the water. It was glorious.

"Hey, daydreamer," Ava called out to me, in a tone anything but gentle, "can you give me a hand with the luggage?"

I put my hands on my hips and slowly turned around to face my accuser. The fact that I had one weekend bag compared to Ava who brought a suitcase appropriate for a month abroad did not occur to her. "Why do you always insist on bringing so many clothes?" I demanded.

She mirrored my hands on hips, ready for a standoff. "Have you ever considered that your petite frame simply requires less material than mine?"

I scoffed.

Ava threw her hands up in a dramatic fashion. "I just never know what I'm going to feel inspired to wear.

Sometimes it's casual and other times I like to dress it up a bit, even with just you girls. Besides, don't play Miss Innocent. You know every time we're away you end up wearing half of what I brought."

I paused for a second. It was true. I never had the patience to plan what to wear for our outings. Plus, I knew what Ava would bring. I could fit into her clothes with just a little extra tug on my corset—she was quite a bit taller yet had an irritatingly small waist. There were many times I would go home after a weekend away with Ava and go in search of one or two items I had grown to love. That was only if she hadn't sneaked them into my bag, of course.

Jo clapped her hands together like a teacher trying to summon her class. "C'mon, you two. Quit your bickering and let's go find Mary!" She had come to think of Mary's as her second home and was thrilled to be back.

Just then, the front door swung open and Mary emerged, looking as lovely as ever. She was some years older than us, but her style made up for it. Her soft, blonde hair never showed an inch of its likely natural gray, and it was always perfectly styled. Her latest hairdo was the short and curly Italian cut, and it really suited her. She might almost be considered plain, except that her modern style always left her looking classy and attractive. Especially impressive was her use of silk scarves, showcasing vibrant colors in her otherwise neutral wardrobe. Plus, they always seemed to pick up the green flecks in her animated, hazel eyes. Today she had on simple beige capri pants and a tailored white cotton blouse, accessorized with one of her gorgeous scarves, this time featuring a turquoise floral pattern.

She squealed and covered her mouth with her hands in a show of excitement. "Girls, you're here at last!"

Ava and I dropped the bags we had been maturely discussing. "Mary!" we shouted in unison, waving madly.

Jo ran to her, in spite of a distance of about ten steps between them. The two embraced. After a minute, Mary disentangled herself to get a good look at Jo.

There was no doubt Mary was pleased with what she saw. "You look even better than I guessed you would: a bona fide career woman. I'm thrilled."

Jo beamed. Mary's opinion of her was more important than anyone else's. "Oh Mary, there just aren't enough ways to say thank you."

Mary cocked her head to the side. "Don't be too quick to thank me. I consider those clothes like an investment. Once you're running the six o'clock news, I will come looking for you to collect my return: a first look at your published works."

Jo blushed. "That's just a dream for now, maybe one day,"

Mary tucked a loose curl behind Jo's ear affectionately. "I have strong faith in you, Jo. But in the meantime, I'd be happy to settle for the latest scoop. I want to know what's going on in Twin Oaks before anyone else.

An insider at the *Twin Oaks Observer* would drive Charles absolutely mad." Mary beamed. "And it would give me unparalleled enjoyment."

Jo saluted her. "Aye, aye, Captain."

She continued to hold Mary's arm affectionately as they walked toward the doorway.

Ava squinted suspiciously as she watched the happy pair. "Isabelle," Ava said, addressing me formally, "I think we're missing some important developments here."

"No doubt," I concurred. "Jo, are you holding out on us? Since when did a junior assistant become privy to breaking news?"

"I may have moved up a little," Jo divulged.

"Don't say any more, Jo!" Ava demanded. "Not until there is a glass of wine in my hand and a comfortable chaise under my rear end."

Jo looked at Ava with a stifled laugh.

Ava raised her eyebrows in response. "What?" she asked innocently, "I just want to be comfortable when I hear all the exciting updates on our new town dweller!"

Mary ushered us inside. "Go on ladies. Put your bags in your rooms and meet me on the back deck."

Chapter 5

Ten minutes later, we gathered on the back deck. Four lounge chairs were set up, overlooking the water. Nearby, there was a table with wine glasses and a variety of finger foods that Mary's housekeeper, Mrs. Collins, was just putting out.

We had known Mrs. Collins almost as long as we had known Mary. During the war, Mary would often have Jo, Ava, and me over for a weekend reprieve from the factory. It was during these tough years that Mrs. Collins got to know us well and often served as a wise and comforting voice to all of us. Her conservative, sensible nature was tempered by a genuine kindness and compassion, which made all four of us hold her dear in our hearts. Of course, that didn't stop us from trying to imitate her heavy Scottish accent and accompanying large, sturdy-framed walk. Each time she caught us in the act, which was often as it was only after too much wine that such feats were attempted, she would shake her head and sigh. Then she always told us the same two things: first, it was better to walk like a bull than talk like a bull, and, second, that we were destined to be friends, as no one in their right minds could ever reach the level of silliness we had achieved on that particular evening—until the next time, of course. We knew she'd forgiven our juvenile antics from the previous evening, however, because the next morning she would always have extra scones and jam out, next to the fresh orange juice and crispy bacon.

Presentation was important to Mrs. Collins and, even for a light snack, the selection was well-planned. A variety of color and texture was used, making it too appetizing to resist. I grabbed a little plate and piled on a selection of seasonal berries, a few cheeses, and some fresh bread. Next to that were several bottles of white wine chilling in a cooler. I filled a glass and looked up at Mrs. Collins who looked pleased by my choices.

"Thank you, Mrs. Collins," I said.

Ava was standing next to me with an equally full plate. "Looks delicious," she added.

Mrs. Collins passed us napkins. "I want to make sure you ladies don't just drink the wine. I have to make the food tempting enough to eat in an attempt to keep some order in the house," she said with just a hint of a grin.

Ava's mouth dropped open in mock indignation. "What on earth do you mean?" she demanded.

"I know too well the sort of trouble you lot get into when you've had too much to drink. I don't want to be wiping shoe prints again off the coffee table after some sort of dance spectacle," Mrs. Collins remarked.

I pointed to Ava and she swiped my hand away pointing right back at me.

Mrs. Collins rolled her eyes. "Some things never change."

Ava and I began to snicker a little, in spite of ourselves.

The patient housekeeper gave my arm a squeeze. "You girls enjoy yourselves now," she said and headed back inside the house.

I looked around, taking in the surroundings again as I sank into my chair. "This is exquisite."

Ava nodded. "Right here is why we never need to go farther than your backyard for our annual getaway, Mary."

"I'm glad you approve," our hostess responded. "Although I can't take any credit for the food, I was instrumental in choosing the wine. And if you don't like it, simply drink more."

Jo leaned forward in her lounger to look at Mary. "You know, it's always a treat to come back here."

Mary tilted her head to meet Jo's gaze. "In your case, Jo, you should think of this as your place, too. After a year of living here, I hope you feel that way by now."

Jo beamed. "Your kindness and generosity is never lost on me. I admit I have come to think of it as a second home."

Ava sat up so quickly she almost launched herself out of the chair. "Can it be my second home, too?"

I closed my eyes, and felt the warm breeze pass by. I could get used to this life: people to make my dinner, clean my house, and do my laundry? Yes, that would be nice. I wondered, if I had this view to look at every day, if I would start to take it for granted.

Ava, who was sitting beside, must've read my thoughts—she was nosy that way. "You and I have a pretty sweet life but every time I visit Mary I feel like a real life princess."

I reached my arms up to stretch. "It's splendid, isn't it?"

"Certainly is. Although it's probably a good thing I don't have all this."

"Do I dare ask why not?" I enquired.

"Well, the way I see it," Ava explained, "if *you* had all this, you would probably read, get involved with charities like Mary does, and use the opportunity to better yourself. You're like that—it's kind of annoying by the way." She winked at me. "I couldn't see myself being nearly so commendable. I think I would probably eat lots of foreign chocolate and become shamefully lazy. My only attempt at bettering myself would probably end at trying to perfect a British accent so I could sound richer and snootier than all those around me. Affected is what they call it, I think."

"The only thing affected around here is your mind," I commented.

Mary overheard the end of our conversation and looked at us quizzically. "Are you two at it again?"

Ava bowed her head in shame. "We simply cannot go anywhere without causing some kind of trouble. I blame Izzy entirely."

I looked at my accuser indignantly. "I should've known the day I met you that you would end up as a perpetual bee in my bonnet."

She stuck her nose in the air and sniffed. "I keep things interesting."

Jo smiled at her. "You are definitely entertaining, '*Rosie*.'"

"Ha! Thank you—" Ava said proudly.

"What did I miss?" Mary interrupted with a freshly topped up glass of wine.

Jo tapped Mary's leg. "Remember Ava's impression of 'Rosie the Riveter' from the factory days?"

Mary smiled widely. "How could I forget? Leave it to Ava to find an American icon who celebrated women with an attitude."

Ava raised her hand. "*And* who represented millions of American women working for the war effort, don't forget,"

"That's true," Mary conceded.

Ava and I adored Rosie. Her poster was plastered all over munitions factories billboards during the war. We spent many nights trying to copy her look: how she did her hair, held a riveting gun, even the way she flexed her muscle. She perfected the art of being cool.

I raised my glass to her. "I'll admit your impression was pretty damned good."

"Thank you, Izzy." Ava nodded, "I know how difficult it can be for you to pay me a compliment."

I flashed her my cheekiest grin. "On the contrary, I love the gesture, especially since the opportunity so rarely presents itself."

Ava pressed her lips together. "Sleep with one eye open tonight, old friend."

I rose above her immaturity and turned toward Jo. "Did Mary say something about you considering trying your hand at becoming a reporter?"

Jo started working at the local newspaper, the *Twin Oaks Observer* almost as soon as she graduated her secretarial course. I figured Mary pulled a few well-connected strings to get her an interview, although it was Jo's own hard work that beat out the other candidates for the job. She prepared for weeks before the job testing, and it paid off: she got a perfect score on the required tests.

Jo's cheeks flushed and her eyes opened wide. "I'm not really sure, at this point. I never saw myself as particularly ambitious, but being on my own seems to be waking up all sorts of new aspirations in me."

I was curious. "Are there any female reporters at *The Observer*?"

Ava reached over and swatted me, giving me, what I called, the stink eye. "Hey, dream crusher, I think I see some kids who don't know about the tooth fairy. Why don't you go harass them?"

I bit my lip. My question came out wrong. "I think it's a wonderful idea. I just wondered if it was realistic."

Jo gave me a sympathetic smile. "Don't worry, Izzy. You're right. It wouldn't be easy. There's not many. But our new managing editor is determined to be a real newspaper, not just a community bulletin. He wants to focus on important issues, as well as local events, and he believes the female readership could play a role in that so he is going to introduce a column devoted to women's interests."

"That sounds promising," I remarked.

Jo sat up excitedly. "It's just at the development stage but he wants to examine the roles of women in society, not just print casserole recipes."

I was impressed. "It certainly sounds encouraging, for you and for us readers, too."

"If it goes well, there may be future opportunities, even for someone like me," Jo explained.

Mary had been listening intently. "That's exciting. Now is the time to pursue your dreams, Jo."

I could see the glint of excitement in Jo's eyes. "Working there makes me feel like I can pursue the stars.

My next assignment is researching female athletes and sport."

Mary looked pleased. "With all the attention Maureen Connolly is getting in the media, it's a good time to focus on it."

I agreed. "They say she's going to be the first woman to win a Grand Slam in tennis."

Ava looked confused. "What's that?"

I turned to her. "It's when a player wins the championship in all four major tournaments around the world. So far, she's won three. If she wins the US Open, she'll have done it."

Ava's eyes widened. "Wow!"

I was eager to discuss it. "It's a huge accomplishment. If she succeeds, it will be a victory for herself and for women, in general."

Ava leaned over and nudged Jo. "Uh, oh, I hear a lecture coming on."

I crossed my arms. "It just seems like, before the war, a more independent spirit was celebrated and accepted for women. There was a higher regard for a woman having her own mind and position. Now there's such a push to go back to just staying at home and tending to the family. If Maureen Connolly succeeds, it will remind the world that women can achieve just as much as any man."

Ava was shaking her head. "You're such a rebel. I don't know how Frank puts up with you sometimes."

I tried to reach over and smack her arm. "Not every

woman can get a man to listen to her the way you do, legs."

Ava shrugged her shoulders. "If someone is disrespecting you, stop talking to them. It's that simple. No one can make you feel inferior without your consent."

I gritted my teeth. "You know, as much as I love Eleanor Roosevelt, her words become quite trying when uttered from your lips."

Ava whipped her head around to look at me. "I would count yourself lucky, then. I have a much tougher burden to bear. There are virtually no words that are uttered from your lips that I don't find trying."

My mouth formed a perfect open circle. "You know, if we weren't in this lovely setting and I wasn't a perfect lady, I'd probably throw you in the pool right now!"

"Heathen!" Ava barked.

As Ava and I started to descend into a plethora of name-calling and animal comparisons, Mary interrupted our discussion. "While your witty banter could keep us amused for the entire evening, I have to insist on going inside. The mosquitoes are even more annoying than the two of you."

Jo chuckled. "I first must commend Izzy's astute observation that Ava knees really do look like that of a chicken!"

With that, Ava chased Jo and me all the way to the door. I think I saw Mary shaking her head with a poorly hidden smile on her face.

Chapter 6

As we were traipsing through the house, still giggling like children, the front door opened. Charles walked in. He was wearing a navy sports coat, matching pants, and a pressed white shirt. The effortless style suited his lean frame. Easily placed in the tall-dark-and-handsome category, it was hard not to notice him. He took a minute to look us over. An expression of surprise then amusement spread across his face.

"Good day, all. I see your ladies' weekend is off to a rousing start."

I felt my cheeks flush. In an attempt to regain some dignity, I tried to compose myself, "Charles, it is lovely to see you again. It has certainly been a while." *Good one, me*, I thought.

"That it has, Isabelle," he replied. "I dare say I don't need to ask how everyone is feeling this evening. I can observe from the flush in your cheeks and the swagger in your step that no one is feeling any pain."

My attempt failed. Mary walked in from behind and came to our rescue. She regarded her husband with a cold gaze. "Charles, don't give the girls a hard time. We're having a positively wonderful time, and we don't appreciate any teasing from you."

Charles pretended to pout. "C'mon now. I'm only having a little fun. It always delights me to see the mischief you get into on these girls' weekends. I only want to join in."

Mary never took her eyes off him. "Your life has no shortage of fun. This is one of the few times you are simply not invited."

"Fair enough," Charles said reluctantly. "I will not interfere but I can't promise to refrain from eavesdropping now and again for nothing other than a silent chuckle. The amusement you ladies provide me after a few cocktails is irresistible."

"That may be. You are not one to resist *anything* that catches your fancy. However, in this case, I must insist you try," Mary responded icily.

Charles's countenance changed and he stiffened at Mary's final comment. He shot her a look that matched her animosity toward him.

Jo looked at Ava and me intently. "You girls want to

come and see the rest of the suits Mary ordered for me?"

I didn't want to be dragged away from observing this intense exchange but followed, nonetheless. Ava and Jo climbed up the stairs toward Jo's room. I stopped short of the staircase and turned around quietly so neither Mary nor Charles could see me. I continued to watch them. There was a thick sense of contempt from both parties.

"My love, if all it took to keep a smile on your face was this lot here, I'd plead with them to never leave," Charles jeered.

Mary took a moment to roll her shoulders back into a proud yet formal posture. "Charles, if you had shown me the loyalty and faithfulness these women had, my smile would've lasted long enough to suit even you, I'm sure. As it stands, I'm quite certain you've found a thousand smiles since, perhaps just none so naive as mine was, even among your youngest conquests."

A condescending smile then spread across Charles' smug face, eclipsing any trace of his natural good looks. "You know I love you as much as I did the day we married."

"Of that, I have no doubt," Mary whispered, the scorn she exuded almost palpable.

Charles opened the door to leave and paused, a low growl delivering his last words, "Why don't you put down that wine glass and try having a cup of coffee for a change. You're embarrassing yourself." Then he strolled out the door as if he hadn't a care in the world.

Mary wasn't letting him go that easily. "Don't you dare walk away from me when I'm talking to you."

He ignored her warning and kept going. She followed him. I peeked out a nearby window. It looked like he was heading to the boathouse. Mary wasn't far behind him, and I could see her anger was growing. Charles continued to pay no attention to her, which I was certain didn't help. He entered the small building and closed the door. Mary tried to follow him in, but he must've locked it because she was unable to turn the door handle. She turned on her heel back toward the house with a determined and furious expression. I'd never seen Mary lose her cool like that before.

I assumed the drama was over and walked down the hall to the nearby sunroom. I exhaled loudly as I collapsed on the mammoth sofa facing out toward the picturesque grounds. What was that all about? Mary and Charles had never acted like newlyweds, but this was way beyond any marital tiff. I could never imagine talking to Frank with such hostility or vice versa. Suddenly this beautiful house I had spent so much time daydreaming about seemed too big. It felt stiff and lonely.

After a few minutes, I began to wonder where everybody had gone. Mary probably wanted a few minutes to compose herself and Ava and Jo were admiring each other's wardrobes, no doubt. I looked around and a large, odd something-or-other caught my eye. I climbed out of the couch I had sunk into and walked over to it. I got a little excited as I recognized the contraption from a magazine ad. A personal vibrator! I always wanted to try one of these. It was the latest and greatest fitness machine, according to all the ads. It looked like a large scale from a doctor's office but it had a thick belt that came out from the top. You placed the belt around your waist or your rear end. The machine then sent out an intense vibration, and it simply jiggled the fat away from the corresponding area. I placed the belt around my waist and turned it on. There was a loud high-pitched buzzing sound, and I felt my whole body begin to shake. What a strange sensation! I wondered how long it would take before I could fit into one of Ava's skirts without the rib-crusher—my tightest girdle.

About fifteen minutes later, an unpleasant squawk filled my ear and my fitness time was interrupted. "What the hell are you doing?" Ava shouted above the buzzing of the machine.

I rolled my eyes. "What does it look like? I'm reducing," I yelled back, trying to push her hand away from the off switch. I failed to stop her and she cut my dream short.

"Why did you do that?" I snapped.

"I'm not even going to dignify that with a response," she said flatly. She turned to get Jo's support who was watching us from the comfy couch.

Jo threw her hands up in a defensive position. "Don't look at me. I'm just a spectator."

I was attempting to unscramble myself from the belt, when Mary walked in. I wanted to ask her about this miracle machine but, when I saw her face, I knew my whittling waist would have to wait. Mary was still flustered and upset.

I bit my lip. "Mary, are you okay?"

She grabbed a bottle of wine assertively. "I'm all right," she muttered distantly through her blotchy, tear-stained face. "I will be even better once we open up this tempting bottle of chardonnay." But her hands were shaking too much to uncork it.

Ava gently took the wine out of Mary's hands, smiled sympathetically at our distressed friend, and, with the twist of a corkscrew, had the wine open in seconds. "You must have been reading my mind."

Jo got up and put her arm around Mary's waist. "I think I have to stick with water for a bit. I might fall asleep otherwise."

Ava was pouring out the wine when I started to ask, "You know Mary, I hate to pry—"

Ava snorted. "Yeah, right."

I shot her a look and she shut up.

"—but I've never seen you this upset," I continued.

"Really, I'm fine," Mary answered. "Charles and I have been going through a rough patch, that's all."

Jo squeezed Mary's waist. "Mary, you don't need to explain anything to us."

Mary put her head on Jo's petite shoulder. "I appreciate that, Jo. The truth is our relationship has been complicated lately and there are some things Charles and I needed to work out. But I took care of it, once and for all," Mary affirmed.

Jo led her to the couch and they sat down.

Ava raised an eyebrow. "Care to expand on that, Mary?"

Mary shook her head. "Not now, it will all become clear in time."

Ava and I joined our friends on the sofa. I had a thousand more questions I wanted to ask but I decided I'd wait until I had time to speak to Mary alone. I wished I could rid myself of a nagging feeling I had at the bottom of my stomach.

To move the focus off Mary and Charles, we began to ask Jo more about her new life.

I had the first question, of course. "What is the best thing about being out on your own?"

Jo looked at us excitedly. "There are a lot of good things. But the first thing I really noticed is *not* being noticed—and it's refreshing."

I was a little confused. "What do you mean?"

"Being from a rural community, I'm used to everyone knowing my business," Jo clarified, "And it's nice to have such a tight-knit circle some of the time. But it's also great to have some freedom. I like going out and not having to tell anyone where I'm going and what time I'll be home. Not that Mary and Charles were like that. But it's different when you have your own apartment."

Ava sat up. "Okay, you've piqued my interest. Where *are* you going? Is someone keeping you out late?"

"Ava," I said with a warning tone.

"What? I'm trying to make the girl feel at home," she said defensively.

Jo giggled. "Unfortunately, it's not that exciting. Mostly I've been staying late at work. I love helping the writers do background for stories. There's a research room we can go to and read reference books and newspaper clippings. They even have years of print on microfiche and it's open to anyone on staff."

Ava slumped back, looking deflated. "We need to take you out, Jo. I think you've forgotten how to have fun."

"For me, it's not just fun, it's engrossing," Jo explained. "I've never had access to that kind of information before. Growing up on a farm, with parents who wanted to shelter us, meant no newspapers, no television, and a very strict watch on the radio programs we listened to. And Kevin was no better. For him, it was more of an issue of control but, either way, it feels like a privilege to have access to all of that stuff now. The more I read, the more I want to learn."

I was impressed. "I can see why you've been moving up so quickly. Finding something you love to do and pursuing a career around it means you never really have to work a day in your life."

Mary had returned back to her calm and collected self. "I just hope you're not giving up on the idea of finding love. If you're so focused on work, can you still make time for socializing and meeting new people?"

Jo raised her eyebrows. "I don't know if I'm ready for that again."

Mary looked at her with motherly concern. "What about your dreams of a marrying a good man and having children? You're only a few years away from thirty."

"I know, Mary. But I feel like I've changed," Jo confessed "One of the reasons I kept trying to make things work with Kevin is that I thought it was my only chance to have a family. But since working at the paper I've heard lots stories of couples having children a little later. I'm not giving up on that dream, but I'm trying not to make it the only one I have."

Mary nodded. "You've grown up so much, Jo. I was never able to have children of my own, and I made peace with it. I'm happy to hear it's not your only focus. But it doesn't mean I'm not going to start setting you up. I happen to know a lot of mature yet eligible bachelors."

Jo groaned.

Ava perked up again. "My guess is there are some handsome reporters walking around the paper, too. They always seem so intelligent and worldly in the movies."

I saw Jo's hesitation. "Would you two stop pressuring the poor woman? It's like a double dose of pushy mom. She'll get there when she's ready."

Jo smiled at me gratefully. "I'm working hard and doing my best. I just don't think I can handle any more right now."

Mary took a sip of wine and regarded Jo. "Love can happen at the most unexpected time. Just don't close the door on it."

"Okay, I won't," Jo promised.

Ava raised her glass for a toast. "I think Eleanor Roosevelt was right when she said, 'Do what you feel in your heart to be right—for you'll be criticized anyway.'"

Jo raised her glass to meet Ava's. "'You'll be damned if you do and damned if you don't.'"

Mary and I raised our glasses and joined in the toast.

Mrs. Collins interrupted our chat to let us know dinner was almost ready.

Mary cleared her throat. "I have a surprise."

I looked at her curiously. "What kind of surprise?"

"I didn't want to mention it before, since you and Ava can be a bit put off about these type of things, but I've asked two of my close friends to join us for dinner. They've been wanting to meet you girls for ages," she announced.

"Fun!" Jo exclaimed, clearly relieved the conversation had moved on from her. "Who's coming?"

"Maggie Connors and Erica Dorner," Mary told her.

"Is that Maggie from the club? She's so nice," Jo stated, looking at Ava and me as if in explanation.

"It is, Jo, and you're right, she is very nice. You've

probably also run into Erica, too. She's Charles's secretary," Mary informed us.

Jo tapped on her head as if it would somehow jumpstart her memory. Apparently, it worked. "Oh, yes, of course! She's a little more reserved so I haven't talked to her as much, but she always *looks* fabulous, I must say."

Mary smiled. "She does, doesn't she? We've bonded over a few shopping excursions we'll have to tell you about. Now—you two aren't going to pout, are you?" she asked, directing her question toward Ava and me.

Ava frowned. "You don't give us much credit, Mary. Any friend of yours is a friend of ours."

Mary sighed. "Ava, I've invited you countless times to the golf club, and you've managed to find an excuse every time. Don't think I haven't noticed. I know you can be a bit wary of an uppity attitude."

"I am sometimes a little uncomfortable around an abundance of wealth, I suppose," Ava acknowledged.

I let a giggle slip out. Ava looked at me suspiciously. "Do you have something to add?"

"Just that you actually told me not too long ago you would rather poke your eyes out with a fork than be forced to sit around and listen to a bunch of self-important rich folks talk," I said, smiling at her openly.

Ava fluttered her eyelashes. "Yes, Izzy, we just went over that. Anything else?"

Mary sighed again. "I'm going to have to grudgingly

defend Ava on this count, seeing as you're almost worse."

Ava silently laughed and pointed.

"What are you talking about? I'm not in Robin Hood's gang of Merry Men," I said innocently.

Mary shrugged. "No, but you avoid formal parties like the plague. Any mention of a grown-up activity and you run for the hills."

I balked at the suggestion.

Mary gave me a stern look. "There's a reason you two are kindred spirits, you know."

I conceded defeat. "Okay, okay. We'll try to keep our savage and impertinent talk at bay."

Ava nodded adamantly. "I concur wholeheartedly and without reserve."

"Just give my friends a chance, please?" Mary appealed to us, "I've wanted you all to meet them for ages."

"Anything for you, Mary," I promised.

"Ditto," Ava stated.

It was a good thing we hashed that out—and not a minute too soon. For a moment later, the door belled rang. It was Maggie Connors.

Chapter 7

Mary went to greet Maggie at the door and then brought her into the sitting room to join us. I guessed she was around Mary's age but looked older. She had short, light-brown curly hair that showed a little graying at the front. She was wearing a navy skirt that went just below her knees and a matching square-shouldered jacket with a white blouse underneath and sensible flat-heeled brown shoes. It was a nicely tailored suit and made of quality rayon but it was outdated and reminded me of the more austere fashion from a few years back where a woman's silhouette was downplayed, quite a departure from the figure-flattering styles of today.

More importantly, though, she had a warm smile and

a kindness about her that made me feel comfortable right away.

After initial introductions, we all relaxed back into our seats.

"Maggie, are you a member of the Twin Oaks Golf Club, too?" I asked.

"I am. My husband and Charles are both golfers and lawyers. They are two of a foursome who play regularly together. It is a passion for them, which means during golf season, Mary and I are often alone at dinner time. As such, we have become quite friendly, preferring the company of each other to that of an empty house."

Mary nodded. "Maggie just lives around the corner, too, so we'll often eat together here or at Maggie's and then go for a long stroll after. It's become rather a good habit, I'd say."

"Yes, one that I've come to look forward to," Maggie said affectionately, "But what I could never figure out until now was Mary's secret to staying young. I was hoping it was those walks and fresh air but now I see the truth: surrounding herself with youth. I think if I had a set of friends like you to keep up with, I'd look a little more bright-eyed myself."

"Maggie," I said, "I'm not sure where you're spending your time, but if we girls are your idea of a young crowd, you need to get out more."

Maggie tapped her cheek. "Come to think of it, the club mostly caters to a fairly seasoned crowd, doesn't it? You may be on to something, Isabelle."

Ava frowned. "Speak for yourself, Izzy," she stated. "I consider myself quite on par with the kids of today. All their talk of being cool and such, I can identify with it."

I chuckled. "Yes, any time you're in the mood for immaturity you need to look no further than Ava. She's maintained it quite remarkably, in fact."

Ava's frown deepened. "Izzy uses her wit so frequently, it's hard to believe she has any wits left at all."

Jo shushed us with a wave. "It gets easier to ignore these two as you spend more time with them," she informed Maggie.

Ava and I looked at her and nodded in agreement.

Another knock on the door brought Erica Dorner. Mary went to greet her, and I took the opportunity to use the facilities near the entrance. Erica was an attractive woman with ash-blonde hair secured neatly in a side bun. She was dressed in stark contrast with Maggie's plain, unassuming style. She was wearing a crimson red dress with black and white details that highlighted her hourglass figure. Matching red high-heeled shoes completed the look. There was also a big difference in her demeanor compared to that of Maggie's. Where Maggie was open and genial, Erica was quieter, though hardly unfriendly. Mary had such a variety of friends, I was actually looking forward to getting to know them better. I scolded myself silently for avoiding dinner parties Mary had invited me to in the past.

When Erica came in, she had some golf clubs with

her. She left them at the door as she accompanied Mary down the hallway. She paused briefly to ask Mrs. Collins to phone William Stormwell at his home and let him know she would be late for their evening meeting. Mrs. Collins did so immediately, giving Erica a few minutes to chat with everyone before dinner. I followed shortly after as Mary was beginning to introduce her.

"Ladies, I'm so happy to have you meet my close friend, Erica. She is Charles's secretary and occasional keeper. Where she finds the patience and fortitude to deal with my husband on a daily basis, I cannot say."

I smiled at her. "Are you a golfer, too, Erica? I saw you brought some clubs with you."

She absently looked at the door where the clubs stood. "I am but those are actually Charles's new clubs. They delivered the clubs to the office only yesterday. He's been so anxious to get them, I thought I'd bring them with me. I went by the boathouse and knocked but there was no answer so I thought I'd bring them up here."

"You're so thoughtful," Mary said.

"And skilled," Ava commented. "How did you manage to carry a giant golf bag full of clubs with no cart in three-inch heels? I'd be wheezing, at best, if I made it at all."

"They're lighter than they look," Erica told her.

"That's unlikely," Mary said. "But between tennis and swimming you're just about the fittest person I know. Speaking of that, Jo, if you have any questions about competitive tennis for your research, Erica here is an excellent reference. Not only was she the captain of the tennis club during college, she also was nicknamed the "stone bullet.""

Jo looked excited. "That is quite extraordinary."

I was curious. "What's behind the name?"

Erica waved her hand as if to push it aside. "Some people found I was hard to read which can make it difficult to anticipate a player's movements. It was silly, really."

"Hardly," Mary disagreed. "Erica actually came close to going pro. Her serve is the fastest and most accurate I've ever seen."

Erica regarded her friend thoughtfully. "You're very kind, Mary. Anyways, I do love the sport so if you have any questions, I'd be happy to give you my two cents' worth."

Jo raised her eyebrows. "Thank you, Erica. That could come in really handy."

"As will Charles's new clubs, I'm sure." Mary grinned. "Charles will be thrilled you brought them over. He ordered those weeks ago and has been more excited than a child waiting for Christmas."

Erica gave Mary a subtle smile. "He has a big game in the morning, and I think he was hoping to get them beforehand."

Maggie glanced over at the new clubs. "Harold has been talking about the round tomorrow for weeks. The men have been giving each other a hard time, trying to get under each other's skin. It's hard to believe they're grownups at times."

Mary glanced out the large window. "Charles likes to spend evenings practicing his swing, hitting balls into the ocean. I'm sure we'll see him doing it tonight." Then she looked out again, this time with more intent. "I'm surprised he wasn't in the boathouse, though. I wonder where he's gone. He was gracious enough to give us the main house for the evening and had planned on finishing off some work." She gave no hint there had been any trouble between them earlier. It struck me as rather odd.

Ava peaked outside, too. "What type of work is Charles doing in the boathouse? He never seemed like the hands-on type of man."

Mary scoffed. "No, Charles doesn't like to get his hands dirty. He set up a proper office in there so he could work without any distractions. Although earlier, I'm pretty sure I saw a bottle of whiskey hidden in his jacket pocket. He pretends he isn't drinking it, and I pretend I don't notice it."

Ava turned to Erica. "You're a very dedicated employee, Erica. Talk about good service."

"Mary and Charles have become more than just employers to me," Erica said. "They're like family."

"And that's why I insisted you join us tonight. Besides, I really wanted you to get to know my best friends," Mary added, "Erica was concerned she'd be intruding on our annual weekend by joining us tonight, but I insisted."

Erica shrugged. "With such a kind offer, how could I say no?"

She went to freshen up and Mary told us a little more about her. When Charles started his firm a few years after college, he partnered with his close friend, William Stormwell, whom he studied with at law school. Erica was a contact that William knew and often used in New York for help with both US and European legal matters. She moved to Twin Oaks not long after and began to work for them.

"Erica and I have become quite close since then," Mary explained. "She and I have bonded over our shared passion for travel. We've even gone to New York together. She has an eye for fashion and knows all the best shops."

Ava perked up as soon as she heard Mary talk about Erica's style. "Aside from being treacherous to walk in, her mile-high stilettos are gorgeous."

"She wears them everywhere she goes. I got Jo and myself almost the same pair," Mary said.

I must have looked apprehensive. Mary dismissed my concerns, "You get used to them, I swear."

"She definitely has that fabulous New York style," Jo said admiringly.

Mary turned to Jo. "Who do you think helped me picked out your suits?"

Erica returned from the washroom and sat down.

Jo looked like she had an idea. "Now that I'm earning my own money, maybe I can join you on one of your weekend jaunts. I would love to see all the ins and outs of our fashion capital."

"We should set a date. I'd love to show you around," Erica agreed.

Mary clasped her hands together and smiled. "Jo, that would be so much fun. Maggie has agreed to join us next time we go, too."

Maggie cleared her throat. "I'll be the one in the plain and sensible shoes."

Erica raised an eyebrow. "Not after you see the shoe boutiques I'll show you."

Maggie looked at Mary. "Should I be worried?"

Mary shook her head. "I think you'll do just fine."

I turned to Erica. "It sounds like you're an expert on New York. I'm going to remember that if *I* ever get the opportunity to go. Is that where you're from?"

"No, I'm from Montreal, Canada," Erica answered. "But I worked for a law firm that had their head office there. They were expanding and needed someone who could step into the role quickly and get it going."

"What a great opportunity! Are you French? I don't hear an accent," I asked.

"No, my mother was French but my father was Austrian. So they compromised and spoke English at home. I consider it my first language, although I speak all three," she explained.

Mary grinned. "You can see why Erica is such a

catch for a firm who works with mostly international clients."

Ava had taken a beginner's French book out of the library recently. She thought she would learn the language before going to Paris next summer. She returned it the next day. I didn't bother to ask how it went.

Ava's brow furrowed and she subtly eyed Erica upon learning the attractive secretary could speak three fluent languages. "Geez, I couldn't even remember how to say hello in French—and I really dedicated myself. That's impressive."

I chose not to mention the twenty-four-hour book loan.

Erica looked at Ava. "Well, I was born into a family where three languages were used. It was natural for me to learn them all so I knew everything going on."

It was hard to tell if Erica was trying to be humorous.

"I would love to learn another language," I said. "Plus, the idea of living in New York City is exciting. Getting a little lost there would be so fun and liberating, especially knowing that, no matter which direction you went, you would always be within an arm's throw of a subway."

Erica nodded. "Very true. By the end of my two years there, I was well acquainted with the city, and it really is world class."

I was curious. "Do you mind my asking what made you come to Twin Oaks? After a few years there I imagine you would've carved out a new life for yourself."

"I agree!" Jo piped in. "Why here?"

"I was ready for a slower-paced, more relaxed life. William spoke so highly of his New England seaside hometown I couldn't resist seeing it for myself. Once I was here, I just never wanted to leave."

Ava winked at me. "Well, from everything I've seen about New York, whether in a movie or a book, I think I'd be ready to come here too. I imagine I would find it too hard to resist the temptations such a large, sophisticated city had to offer."

I sighed. "I hesitate to ask what you mean?"

She smiled mischievously. "Well, as a single woman with nobody to answer to, nobody to recognize me, surrounded by well-dressed, sharp-witted men cruising on Wall Street—I'm just saying that I could see trouble."

We all laughed but I saw a brief smile exchanged between Erica and Mary that gave me pause to wonder if there was more to the story then they told us.

Dinner was served a few minutes later in the dining room. It was a delicious roast with all the fixings: potatoes, fresh bread, veggies, and pudding. Nobody made a better dinner than Mrs. Collins.

As we enjoyed the hearty meal, conversation moved on to places we'd like to see and the charms each had to offer. It was nice to hear first-hand accounts of some of the places I'd always dreamed of visiting. Mary was the only friend I'd ever really known who had traveled, but

Erica had been many places, too. It was nice hearing new stories I hadn't heard before.

I guessed by the animated look on Jo's face, she was full of questions. "Of all the places you've been, Erica, where is your favorite?"

"Oh, that's an easy question to answer: Giverny, in France."

I was disappointed I hadn't heard of it. "Where is that?"

"It was Claude Monet's garden sanctuary where he lived and painted for many years. It's the subject of several of his paintings," she informed us.

"It sounds pretty," I said.

"It's magnificent," Erica corrected.

"What makes it so great?" I asked, intrigued.

"Close your eyes and imagine a huge property with an elegant pond and elaborate gardens as far as the eye can see. It's quite breathtaking," she recounted.

Ava sighed. "That does sound beautiful. He has some wonderful paintings."

I nodded emphatically. "I adore his art work so going to see the inspiration for it would be amazing."

"I think so. I'm actually going back to see it again next month," Erica confided with a subtle excitement.

"How lucky," Jo gushed.

"Well, it won't be all pleasure. I'll be in Paris with Mr. Stormwell on business. He speaks no French so he brings me as a trusted interpreter. It's a nice arrangement, and he always gives me an extra day or two to enjoy the sights."

Jo's mouth dropped. "Boy, do I ever wish I had language skills."

"Well, if you ever want to learn, I'd be happy to help. It would be a good exercise to practice my grammar," Erica offered.

Ava waved at Erica. "Can you teach me in time to join you on your excursion? I don't take up much space and I'm happy to carry the luggage."

I imagined Ava as a luggage handler. "Ha!" was all I could muster.

As our discussion shifted, I noted to myself I had to learn more about Giverny and would be visiting the library in the next few days to do just that. Moving on to Paris, London, and various other places, I was lost in a daydream of destinations I must one day visit.

Mary broke up the conversation. "I hate to interrupt what I can see is the beginning of a fun discussion but we should continue our evening in the sunroom. It's a great place to watch the sunset."

Erica was the first one to stand. "I've thoroughly enjoyed my time with you ladies but I'm afraid I am due at William's, and I don't want to get there with a headache, which is guaranteed if I have one more drink. "

Mary rose from her seat and grabbed Erica's hand. "Of course."

Erica squeezed her hand. "Thank you."

Maggie also got up. "I need to be getting home, as well. It's been a wonderful evening. Thank you all so much for including me."

"You are both very welcome," Mary declared. "Maybe now that you've all had a chance to meet, I can convince my young friends here to join us at the club and shake things up a bit."

I couldn't help but laugh. "The notion of us stirring the pot is too tempting to resist. I'd love to."

"I second that notion," Ava agreed. "An evening out with a group of fabulous women is certainly worth getting all dolled up for."

Jo grabbed Mary's arm. "Just make it on a weekend so I can come!"

Mary looked pleased. "Absolutely."

We all said good night and escorted Erica and Maggie to the door. Maggie insisted on walking and set off on foot, waving goodbye. Erica then drove away in a cherry red convertible. The rest of us made our way into the sunroom.

Chapter 8

Mary brought out some of our favorite board games. We all agreed on Monopoly. It was a beautiful evening and the view from the sunroom was superb. We could see the gardens to the left, the impressive boathouse to the right, and the rocky edge of the property where it dropped down to meet the sea.

Ava gazed out at the boathouse. "It's the size of a small home and seems to get bigger every year. I mean we've never even seen the inside!"

I had to agree. "Do you really think Charles actually gets any work done in there?"

Mary smiled. "He does. The place is really not that interesting. When we first got the house, it was a fairly basic room with stairs leading down to the dock where the boat is kept. But after a few years, Charles felt he needed his own space to have peace and quiet. He often works at home, so he built an office and library where he can escape to when he wants to be alone. He calls it his private retreat. We've agreed that, when he's there, he should only be called upon in an emergency."

"Please never mention this to my husband," Ava said, "Next thing you know our garden shed will have a lock on the door with a sign reading 'Men only.'"

I giggled. "It does seem to be a universal dream for men to have some private space where they can do whatever it is they do."

Jo crinkled her nose. "What do you think they want to do in it?"

Ava scoffed. "Nothing you'd read about it any romance novel," she answered confidently. "My guess is most would want to drink, think about sports, and make unpleasant sounds and smells with their bodies. If Bruce ever managed to convert our shed into a man-only room, he would certainly not need a sign to keep me away. My only concern is that I'd rarely ever see him. Now that we're talking it through—"

I had to cut her off. "Ava, you are spoiled with love and attention from Bruce. Besides, don't get any ideas. If Bruce got one, then I'd lose Frank too! No, this man room must remain a secret."

Mary was nodding to confirm our suspicions. "Charles will spend entire evenings in there," she admitted. "Like tonight, he may not emerge until long after we've gone to bed."

Ava and I looked at each other. Our curiosity was unabated. However, we opened a new bottle of wine and started playing Monopoly. We focused on the game and forgot all about the curious idea of a man room. Ava always seemed to win at board games, and I was determined to stop her. All other trains of thought were paused as my competitive streak took over. It was close to midnight as Jo cleaned most of us out of our money and property.

I looked around at my friends and realized I was probably as bleary eyed as they were. It was time to get some sleep. Ava and I were sharing a room so we bid goodnight to Mary and Jo and headed upstairs.

Ava sat on the bed and yawned. "What a fun evening."

I agreed. "I love these girls' weekends. They're so much fun."

Ava inquired if I wanted to use the washroom first to get ready for bed. I smiled at her mischievously.

She cringed in response. "What are you up to? And don't bother to tell me nothing. I can read it all over your face."

"You know me too well," I admitted, attempting to give her my most winning smile. "Okay, I would love to just take a five-minute stroll down to the water. I'm not the least bit tired, all of a sudden. Besides, the moon and stars are calling us, and it's a beautiful night."

Ava rolled her eyes. "Why did I agree to share a room with you? I always forget your tendency to remain unaffected by late nights and too much wine."

"There's something wrong with me," I conceded. "Wine energizes me. It's not my fault. It's a curse!"

Ava sighed. "Yes, a curse on me! By now, I know, of course, that if I don't go, you'll be tossing and turning as well as ignoring repeated requests to be quiet and go to sleep. So, with that, I will say yes, let's take a midnight stroll."

I giggled. "No wonder you're my best friend in the whole world. Who else could put up with me?"

"I consider it a contribution to humanity," Ava groaned. "Now zip it and let's get going before I fall asleep talking about it."

It felt like we were back in high school. We tried not to make a sound as we quietly slipped out the back door.

The night was splendid. The air felt fresh and cool. Summer nights in Twin Oaks could sometimes be almost as humid as the days, but down near the water, there was usually some relief.

We walked down to the edge of the property and sat on the rocks overlooking the ocean. The moon and the stars seemed extra bright tonight. We sat quietly for a few minutes, then I thought I had better make sure Ava wasn't falling asleep here. "How are you feeling?"

"It's such a beautiful night I'm not annoyed with you anymore so you're off the hook."

"I feel fuzzy," I whispered.

Ava giggled. "Izzy, what does that even mean?"

I giggled too. "I'm not accustomed to drinking countless glasses of wine any more. It means my mind is feeling anything but sharp, I suppose."

"Wouldn't the word 'dull,' or even 'tired,' be more accurate then?"

"Well, no, not exactly." I paused. "My mind isn't moving quite as slowly as 'dull' would suggest. And I'm still not feeling all that tired, although I am feeling less energetic. The thoughts in my head are just a little disjointed and incomplete—I think I should stop talking now."

"No, no, unfortunately I completely understand. I don't know whether it's a consequence of an accurate description by you or, more likely, that I've known you too long, but I get it," Ava said.

We looked at each other and smiled. "I think I can sleep now," I told her.

She looked up at the sky. "Thank the Lord."

As we walked toward the back door, a light caught my eye. It was coming from the boathouse. My curiosity was aroused. I looked at Ava momentarily then looked away. I wasn't going to say a word. Ava had put up with enough of my antics tonight.

Then Ava looked at me and sighed. "I see it too."

I pretended I didn't know what she meant. "Pardon me?"

"The light, Izzy. I know you see it. I see it, too. We both want to know what Charles is doing and why he's doing it in the middle of the night."

"Fine, I see it. You have to admit it is odd. After spending all evening alone in there, what could he possibly be up to now? Is he that dedicated to work?"

"If I was a gambler, I'd put my money on no, he's not. Let's go check it out—quietly and discreetly, of course," she suggested.

I agreed eagerly. My desire to sleep was chased away by my innate curiosity. "I'm in."

We slowly made our way over to the boathouse and crept up to a small window where the light first caught our eye. Our heads were so close together they were practically touching. We peered in. There was a cozy look to the place. Bookshelves lined the near wall across from a couch and table. On the far side of the room there was a desk sitting under another window that overlooked the ocean, where a small lamp sat, giving off a low light that filled the room. There was a set of stairs at the far end of the room I assumed must lead down to the dock where the boat was kept.

What a great space for an office, I thought. It was quiet and secluded with ample space and a view of the ocean and surrounding trees.

Then I saw it.

There was a body lying next to the stairs. Ava gasped and my stomach turned over. We ran to the door. It was unlocked, and we rushed in.

Charles Whitmore lay dead in a large pool of blood.

Instinctively, I took in the scene. Charles was lying in an unnatural way, more twisted than at peace. There was a large amount of blood pooled under his body. I guessed it was a chest wound that killed him, as this was where the largest amount of blood seemed to come from. He was wearing trousers and a collared blue shirt, a smart outfit in different circumstances. The most disturbing detail was an expression of shock frozen on his face, a look I couldn't have imagined, even in my darkest nightmares.

There was an open bottle of scotch and a tumbler on a coffee table across from the small sofa on the other side of the room. Next to the whiskey lay a bunch of papers, which I assumed must be work documents since they were typed on legal-sized paper and lying in an organized manner. There was also a bottle of wine with two glasses next to it. Other than that, I couldn't see anything that looked out of place or in any way disturbed. Then something caught my eye from under the desk. I looked closer and my heart sank. Ava must've seen it, too, for she grabbed me suddenly and looked at me with an expression of alarm. The shimmering diamond ring we were looking at was unmistakable. It was Mary's.

"Let's go call the police," I murmured.

"I don't think we should leave him," Ava whispered.

"Ava, there's nothing we can do to help him. C'mon," I urged as I tugged her hand.

She followed as I led her out of the room and closed

the door. The effects of booze evaporated as my mind and heart raced. We walked back to the house in complete silence.

Chapter 9

An hour later, we were sitting in the living room answering questions from the police. I looked across the room and saw Jo holding Mary's hand. The gesture was not enough to stop Mary from trembling. A far cry from her usual demeanor, she looked pale and weak. I wished I could stop answering questions and get these strangers out of Mary's house. There were four police officers here with us, three, in uniforms and the last one in a suit. One uniformed officer was talking quietly to Mary and Jo, a second to Ava, and the third stood near the doorway. All three looked very young. The officer in the suit, Detective Jones, was sitting just inches away from me, on the coffee table, as if the couch across from me was too far. He was more seasoned. I guessed he

got ready in a hurry to come here, most likely pulled
away from his bed, since his short, dark hair looked barely combed through, and his wrinkled brown suit looked
as if he picked it up off the floor. He spoke softly but his
eyes had a steely determination in them, which contra-
dicted the sense of calm he was trying to assert. I
might've thought him ruggedly handsome in other circumstances. I wondered if he knew that, right now, the
words he was speaking to me couldn't be heard over my
wandering thoughts and my pounding heart.

"Mrs. Walsh?" he asked, looking at me.

Damn it, could *he* read my thoughts, too? "Pardon
me?" I answered, trying to open my eyes wider.

"Please focus, ma'am. I asked you what caused you
to go look in the window of Mr. Whitmore's boathouse in
the first place."

"Oh, yes, sorry. We saw a light and we were curious
as to what he was doing up so late."

"And why were you and Mrs. Russell up so late?"

"We were getting some fresh air before heading up
to bed."

"I see. Now, I want you to think back. Close your
eyes and picture the boathouse again as you approached
it. Did you see anyone? Perhaps hear something that you
didn't pay attention to at the time?"

I did as he asked and closed my eyes. I tried to think
about the moments leading up to looking in the window
and finding Charles. But I couldn't concentrate. All I

could do was hear everyone talking. It was too loud. I was too tired. My head felt like it was one big bruise. Ouch.

"I'm sorry, Officer. I'm feeling overwhelmed right now. My thoughts are anything but clear and fresh," I said.

"I understand. It's been a big shock and a long night. I've got the basic facts here," he concluded.

I looked at Ava. She looked as bad as I felt. I guessed the conversation she was having was about as productive as mine. Her blank and bleary eyes told me her thinking hat had fallen off some time ago. Detective Jones must've shared my observation. He wrapped things up quickly, instructing his fellow officers to head out and let us get some sleep. Before he left, he gave us some brief yet clear instructions.

"Ladies, I want you to do only one thing until I see you again. That is rest. I don't want you to discuss what happened or what you saw. Just get some sleep and have a nice, hearty breakfast when you wake up. Two officers will be here all night to make sure no one comes in and no one leaves. In case you missed it, my name is Detective Jones and I will be in charge of this investigation. I will be back early tomorrow and I expect, once you're feeling better, we will get some answers and figure this all out. Do you understand?"

I looked at my friends and nodded. They nodded too. We walked him to the front door and he and his fellow officers left. We regrouped in Mary's bedroom. Jo insisted Mary get under the covers and we all sat around her on the king-sized bed.

"Mary, do you want me to stay with you?" Jo asked.

"No, Jo, I'm okay. I'm going to take a sleeping pill. It'll knock me out. I just wish it would prevent me from waking up to this nightmare."

I wave of sympathy shot through me. "I am so sorry, Mary. What can we do? What do you need?"

"I'm just glad you girls are here. There is nothing to do but what the detective said. Let's get some sleep."

Ava gave Mary a sleeping pill she found in the bathroom and a big glass of water.

Mary swallowed the pill. "Thanks Ava," she said gratefully.

"You're welcome. Now stop hovering around her, girls, and let her sleep," Ava instructed as she ushered us out of the room.

We bid Mary goodnight and closed her door.

"I don't know if I'm going to be able to sleep," Jo said as we stood in the hallway.

Ava rubbed her back gently. "Just climb into your bed and close your eyes, Jo. Trust me, you'll sleep as soon as you lie down. It's been an exhausting night and your body will know what to do."

"Okay, I'll try. Goodnight." Jo disappeared into her room.

Ava and I looked at each other and headed down the

hallway in silence. We climbed into our adjoining beds, and I switched off the bedside lamp. I turned my head and looked at Ava, who I could see quite clearly with the bright moonlight coming in through the window. She was looking up at the ceiling, tears streaming down the side of her face. This was the first time I had seen her cry in years and it made me shudder.

"Ava?" I pleaded.

"Izzy, this is bad. I'm scared," she confided.

I wanted to comfort her. "It's going to be okay. We'll find out what happened, and it will be okay."

Ava turned and looked at me. "That's what I'm afraid of, Izzy. What if finding out what happened is what's going to make it anything *but* okay?"

"Ava, we're both tired and confused," I cautioned.

"So you're thinking it too, huh?" Ava whispered.

"No, I'm not. Mary isn't capable of—" I couldn't bring myself to finish the sentence, "Besides, she was with us all night, wasn't she?"

"Well, yes—except for about half an hour when she wasn't," Ava uttered in a sheepish voice.

I didn't respond. I closed my eyes, thought back to earlier in the evening—which at this point felt like it had occurred weeks ago—and realized Ava was right. Dammit. I had no doubt Mary was innocent of any wrongdoing, yet I really wished right then Mary had not disappeared for so long.

"Izzy," Ava hissed. "Do not give me the cold shoulder. I know Mary is innocent too." Ava's ability to read my mind was really quite remarkable. "I was just playing the devil's advocate!" she continued. "Besides, I'm more cynical than you, always have been. Not my fault!"

"Would you please be quiet? I'm trying to think here for a sec. And don't feel guilty. Mary and Charles had a strained relationship at best. A fleeting thought questioning whether Mary was involved is only reasonable. As long as you dismiss it, there's no need to fret over it. You, Jo, and I know Mary better than anyone in this world. I'm not worried about *us* having doubts of Mary's innocence. It's the rest of the world, the police in particular, that worries me more."

"We may be jumping way ahead of ourselves. The detective was very friendly and seemed more concerned about Mary than anything else, least of all suspicious. He was quite soothing," Ava argued.

"That's what I thought too. But there was something in his face that suggested less sympathy than if Mary was just a straightforward crime victim. He seemed to befriend her, but it was different from the way the officers used to come and inform us about the loss of our loved ones during the war. He kept scanning the room, his eyes constantly wandering, as if he were looking for something. It made me uneasy."

"Now that you mention it, I noticed that too. I just thought he was taking in the beauty of Mary's house. What a fool I am."

"Let's just be careful in our answers and talk to Mary before he gets here."

"You're right. Until we know his thoughts on Charles's death, we shouldn't offer too much information," she said.

I heartily agreed. I was not sure if Ava kept talking after this because I must've fallen asleep. For, the next thing I knew, Jo was in our room, waking us for breakfast.

Chapter 10

It was only seven a.m. when Jo woke us up. I didn't think I'd be able to sleep at all but, at some point, my exhaustion must've overpowered my spinning thoughts and I finally settled. Although I didn't feel great, it was certainly an improvement from when I crawled into bed last night.

"I hope it's not too early for you two. I know it was a late and stressful night but I couldn't sleep. I waited as long as I could bear it before barging in here," Jo confessed. She was visibly anxious, biting her nails and jumping at the slightest noise.

I patted her hand. "Jo, don't worry about waking us early. Sleep is not the top priority right now. Where's Mary?"

She continued gnawing on her nails. "She's making coffee. She said she didn't want to talk until we were all together."

"Why?" Ava inquired.

Jo shook her head. "I don't know. When I got up, she was already bathed and dressed. When I asked her how she's holding up, she said fine but instructed me not to ask any questions until the four of us were sitting down to breakfast."

I got butterflies in my stomach. It wasn't like Mary to be so mysterious. She was as open and direct as anyone I knew.

"Okay, guys, let's not keep her waiting. Let's go," I instructed. I smoothed my hair back with my hand and put a hair band in it to keep it out of my eyes. I didn't want to miss a thing today. I quickly brushed my teeth and was ready to go. Ava was just as fast getting ready, and we were downstairs five minutes later.

Mary was waiting in the sitting room. She had tea, coffee, and various breakfast goodies arranged on the coffee table. Normally such a delectable array of pastries would send me into an immediate place of happy thoughts, but not today. The room felt very different than it had twenty-four hours earlier. The excited giggles and lighthearted exchanges had been replaced by a heavy silence that filled the room. I had the urge to run. This scene reminded me too much of the past: the darkest days of the war when one of us had received word that a loved one was lost across the sea. I poured myself a coffee and sat ready to listen. Ava was beside me and, on the sofa across from us, Jo had taken a seat next to Mary.

Mary looked at each one of us. "There is something I need to tell you and I want you to hear it from me before it comes out publicly."

I looked quickly at Ava and back at Mary. "You can tell us anything, Mary. Nothing would break our loyalty to you."

"We're not here to judge you," Ava added. "We're here to support you."

Mary smiled sadly. "I appreciate that. I really do. I'm going to need that too, because I have a feeling that things are going to get pretty ugly in the next little while. You see, I told Charles last night that I intended to divorce him."

"When? He locked you out of his office—I saw you storm away when you couldn't get in," I admitted.

"I grabbed the spare key and went back. I sure wish I hadn't," she said wistfully.

Jo looked confused. "I'm sorry, Mary, I don't understand. I lived here over a year and rarely saw an ill word between you. Yesterday's argument seemed totally out of character."

Mary sighed. "That's because I had convinced myself I could live with certain things, and I finally realized very recently that, in fact, I could not. You see, girls, Charles has, excuse me, *had* a hard time resisting the desire to stay young."

Ava shrugged her shoulders. "That's not the worst quality in the world. It sounds kind of fun."

"It reminds me of Peter Pan," I added, feeling confused.

"You're both right. It *was* very fun at times and he *is* like Peter Pan in a way. The problem is while Peter Pan doesn't age, Wendy does," she explained.

I nodded. "And you're Wendy, of course."

"Yes, Izzy, that's right. Unfortunately, Charles needed more than just one 'Wendy' to keep him feeling young and amused," she added dryly. "It seems I grew up very quickly, as well. It didn't take long in the marriage before Charles was looking for the next girl to capture his interest. No one held it for long but then he would be on to the next."

"Mary, that's terrible," I remarked.

Ava shook her head. "What a cad."

"I'm sorry, I had no idea," Jo admitted.

I nodded. "None of us did. How could we have been so oblivious to your pain?"

"I had myself convinced it was a character flaw I could live with," Mary replied. "That he is just a man and all men would behave in such a way given the chance. So I tried to ignore it and pretend it didn't bother me."

Ava shook her head. "How could you put up with it for so long? Why not leave before?"

I turned to Ava. "Think of the scandal that would cause."

Mary sat back in her seat. "Actually, I've never worried too much about what others thought."

Ava leaned in. "Money?"

Mary waved her hand in a way that dismissed the suggestion. "I'm an independently wealthy woman. I've always made sure to keep control of that."

Jo gently rubbed her knee. "Then why didn't you leave, Mary?"

Mary looked at each one of us and then cast her eyes on the floor. It suddenly dawned on me why Mary stayed with a playboy husband.

"You were still in love with him," I concluded.

"Yes, Izzy. In spite of his indiscretions, I never stopped loving him. And, in his own way, I think he loved me, too. I entertained the thought of a divorce to try and regain some power, some dignity. I don't know if I would've actually done it. But I didn't want to make an empty threat so I got a lawyer. I told myself I was prepared to go through with it if Charles refused to stop acting like an ass, once and for all. I bring this up to you all now because yesterday, when I went back to the boathouse, I told him."

"I'm guessing it didn't go over very well?" I asked.

Mary shook her head. "That's an understatement. He flew into a rage. He said he wouldn't have it. I was his wife and it wasn't up to me to say otherwise. He was the man of the house and such decisions were his and his alone. I was drunk and angry and told him I hadn't loved him in years—that he was a pathetic excuse for a man. Then I told him I had a lawyer. He told me he'd divorce me over his dead body. I said whatever it takes I would do to be free of him. Then I took my ring off, threw it in his face and stormed out."

Jo had tears in her eyes. "Oh, Mary."

Mary sighed. "I just can't believe that was the last conversation we will ever have. I can't take back what I said. I hate myself for that. I miss him already, and, in spite of everything, he was the love of my life."

We were all quiet for a minute. I think we just needed a second to process what Mary had just told us.

I looked at Ava for help. I just didn't know what to say. She met my gaze and put her hand over mine. The gesture comforted me. "You and Charles were together a very long time," Ava reminded Mary. "I'm sure he knew you loved him. If you didn't, you wouldn't go through the trouble of divorcing him. It was a desperate threat to *regain* his love and attention, not to lose it."

Mary looked hopeful. "Maybe you're right."

Ava's reassuring words spread and I regained my faculties. "Did you tell all this to the police last night?"

"Most of it, I did. The detective told me not to leave here until they had time to do an autopsy." Mary held her head in her hands. "My poor Charles."

Ava's eyes darted around the room. She took a deep breath in. "Mary," she commanded. "We're all shocked and upset by Charles's death. But we need to throw some concern your way. Charles didn't look like he died from natural causes, or even an accident."

The recent widow looked confused. "What are you saying, Ava? Do you think that Charles was murdered?"

Ava hesitated. I nodded at her as if to tell her I was okay now. I took the reins to answer Mary's question. "We don't want to draw an early conclusion, but something happened in that room that I don't think Charles was, in the least bit, prepared for."

Before our conversation could continue, there was a sharp knock at the door. It was Detective Jones. Two uniformed officers accompanied him.

"Good morning Detective Jones," Mary said, "I hope you are here to tell us more about what happened to my poor husband."

"I would think you already know, Mrs. Whitmore," he stated.

"I'm afraid I don't understand," Mary replied.

"Mary Whitmore, you are under arrest for the murder of Charles Whitmore." He stood aside and two uniformed officers approached Mary with handcuffs.

Ava instinctively tried to block the officers from reaching Mary. "Are you out of your bloody minds?"

I stepped in quickly and grabbed a hold of Ava before she collided with the officers. "Ava, please."

She glared at me but acquiesced. As the uniformed officers put the handcuffs on, the detective read Mary her rights.

I tried to reason with him. "Detective Jones, what Ava means is that Mary is not a killer. She simply would not be capable of such an act. You cannot possibly believe with any confidence that she murdered her husband."

"Where there's smoke there's fire. Plain and simple. I don't argue with the facts." He turned to the uniformed officers. "Let's head out, lads."

"What facts?" I persisted desperately.

"I am not at liberty to discuss that, Mrs. Walsh. If you would like to come down to the station and talk to me later today, please do."

With that, the detective gestured to the uniformed officers to take Mary away and, in the blink of an eye, she was being led out in handcuffs. Jo, Ava, and I were left gaping at the scene in front of us. Mary was put in the back of a police car, and she stared at us through the window, pleading for help with just the look of fear in her eyes.

I ran out and addressed the detective one more time. "Detective, what can we do to help Mary?"

He looked at me grimly. "Like I said, come down to the station later today. Tell us everything you can about the Whitmore's relationship as well as anything else that you think may be pertinent." He paused. "But first and foremost, I would recommend getting your friend a good lawyer."

With that, he got into his car. We were left feeling

shocked and powerless to help our friend, who was being driven away down the long, winding driveway.

Chapter 11

Although still feeling a little numb from the events that took place, my mind went on autopilot, and I started to think about what we should do next. With no complaints today about me being a little too bossy, Jo and Ava listened to my plan of action with no argument. I told Jo I would drop her off with Ava and they could fill Bruce in about what happened. They would need to be ready for me to pick them up in an hour. I would go home, call Mary's lawyer, and then talk to Frank. We needed to stay focused and strong to figure this out—and for Mary's sake, we needed to do it quickly.

We were about to leave Mary's house when a taxi pulled up and Mrs. Collins got out. She looked worried and sad as she approached us. "Where's Mary?" she demanded, without any sort of greeting.

"Mrs. Collins, I need you to sit down and listen," I cautioned.

"I've been sitting on my rump for two hours at the police station. I won't sit another minute. Now tell me, where is Mary?" she repeated fiercely, looking at the house and then at me.

"Mary is on her way there, I'm afraid. The police just arrested her for Charles's murder," I answered plainly.

She looked at all three of us and cupped her hand over her mouth, as if trying to stifle a cry. "It's all my fault. They arrested her because of me." She then began to sob.

I led Mrs. Collins to a bench near the front entrance of the Whitmore's and insisted she sit down. "Please tell us what you are talking about," I entreated while trying to sooth her.

She drew in a deep breath and paused. "This morning, at the crack of dawn, the police came to my door and asked me to come down to the station to answer a few questions. I obliged, of course, and they informed me, once I was there, that Mr. Whitmore was dead. I had no time to absorb the shock of the news before they started peppering me with questions about the Whitmore's marriage. In truth, I didn't have much to say. But it took me a few minutes before I realized they were asking in a way that showed they were suspicious of Mary," she explained.

"It doesn't sound like you added to any suspicions they didn't already have," I told her.

"You didn't let me finish, lass," she maintained. "After the questions about the Whitmore's marriage, they showed me a ring and asked if it was Mrs. Whitmore's. I confirmed it was. Only then, did they seem satisfied with my answers. They let me go after that. I knew I must've said something to get Mary in trouble because not two minutes passed before I saw a whole crew of them leave together in a way that I knew meant business. I took a taxi straight over here but, obviously, I was too late."

Ava bent down and looked directly into Mrs. Collins eyes. She seemed to want to make sure the caring housekeeper listened to her words. "They would've found out the ring was Mary's one way or another. You've done nothing wrong, Mrs. Collins."

"But at least she would've had more time to prepare. I could've warned her they were looking at her for this tragedy."

Ava kept at Mrs. Collins's eye level. "I don't think you can really prepare to be arrested for murder. It's not like planning for a trip abroad."

A thought occurred to me. "There was nothing you could do then, but there is now. Can you help me find her lawyer's phone number? I need to alert him right away."

"Of course, come with me," she instructed.

Having a task seemed to calm Mrs. Collins's nerves. She took out a handkerchief, wiped her tears, and set off toward the house. She signaled for me to follow and I did. She left last night only after the kitchen was back in order following dinner, so the house was still as clean and tidy as she had left it. It was clear she was in full charge of this part of the house because it was more organized than anywhere else in the house. Not a thing was out of place. In no way did it resemble my kitchen. She walked straight over to a drawer and opened it. The Rolodex was out and the lawyer was called within minutes. I breathed a little easier with that done. We bid Mrs. Collins a temporary goodbye and left the house. I dropped off Ava and Jo and, fifteen minutes later, I opened my front door.

Frank was dressed casually in light wool pants and a short-sleeved cotton shirt. He briefly glanced up from reading the paper. "What are you doing home? Aren't you supposed to be staying at Mary's until tomorrow?" When I didn't answer, he looked at me again, this time a little longer. "Geez, I don't know if it's what you drank or how much, but you're looking a little rough this morning, Izzy. Maybe you should've slept in a bit longer to combat that wine," he teased.

I burst into tears. He dropped the paper and came over to where I stood. Although not particularly tall, he could still wrap his strong arms around me in a way that always made me feel protected. I could smell the aftershave as his smooth face brushed past my ear. After a firm hug, he held my sagging frame out to take a closer look.

His kind, hazel eyes scanned me hastily and he smiled sympathetically. "Izzy, you just need a shower. You know I think you're beautiful no matter what. You'll look and feel better in a jiff. The kids are out in the backyard and I'll even banish them from the house for a few hours so you can have a nap."

The idea of making things better with a simple nap just made me cry harder. Frank stopped talking for a minute and held me tighter. It was rare for me to cry. He stroked my hair in a further effort to calm me down. I allowed myself to stay like that, feeling safe and secure, just for a minute.

I pulled myself together and told him. "Charles is dead, Frank." Just hearing those words come out of my mouth sent a chill down my spine. I hadn't yet spoken them.

Frank stiffened and pulled away from me so he could look in my eyes. He fumbled his words, "Dead! What— What happened?"

"The police think Mary killed him. They just arrested her!"

Frank stared at me. He still looked stunned as he tried to read my face. "That's preposterous. When did this happen, Izzy? Why didn't you call me?"

"It just happened. There's been no time, Frank. I just called her lawyer from her house. Now I need to get to jail to see her. I don't have any more time to talk right now," I said, feeling overwhelmed.

"Whoa, Izzy. You need to slow down. First, I want you to go lie down. Then have a shower. I'll put on a pot of coffee. You're not going anywhere until you have calmed down and are able to think straight. You will not be any help to Mary in the state you're in right now."

I had to admit, with the recent events racing through my mind, I was struggling to return to the rational and collected way my thinking normally worked. I decided Frank may be right and I went into our bedroom. It was cool and dark. I practically melted under the covers. I fell asleep for what felt like three hours but was, in actuality, only about twenty minutes. I woke up and hopped into the shower. The short nap and hot shower helped my senses wake up. I was feeling a little more prepared for the ordeal lying ahead.

I walked into the kitchen and Frank had the coffee and some of my favorite biscuits out ready for me. This small gesture made me remember why I loved this man. He was sitting at the table, patiently waiting to hear what had happened. With as much clarity as I could muster, I told him the events of the night. There were a few times, he had to slow me down, and he asked a few questions, but mostly he just sat and listened. When I was through, I felt a little better. Relating the story to Frank made me go over the night with a clearer head. It was rare that I spun into a panic, but this morning was definitely one of those times. I was much calmer and I felt thankful for that. I needed a lucid mind now, perhaps, more than ever before.

Feeling more confident, I headed out. Frank would take the kids out for ice cream and over to the park. That pretty much gave me the rest of the day to focus solely on the task ahead. It took me up until now to figure out what exactly that meant. I realized as I drove back to pick up my friends that the best way to help Mary was to figure out who killed Charles Whitmore. Only once we knew who the real killer was, would Mary be absolved of any wrongdoing in his death.

Chapter 12

Jo and Ava were as anxious to go see Mary as I was. When I arrived to pick them up at Ava's, they were ready to go. Bruce was waiting with them, but there was no trace of his usual laid-back smile. In its place, there was a furrowed brow and a grave expression clearly seen, even behind his thick, dark-rimmed glasses. I often liked to tease him about being the real-life Clark Kent because he resembled Superman's alter ego, but today neither he nor I were in the mood for our usual banter.

I wasn't surprised Bruce was close by. He was fiercely protective of Ava and never liked to see her upset. There were a few times in the past he had to defend her from those she had upset, usually with her liberal politics. Luckily, in spite of his mild-mannered demeanor, he had the build of an athlete so no one ever wanted to challenge the beefcake behind the firecracker. Little did they know he only looked the part, spending most of his days crunching numbers, rarely lifting anything more than Ava's frequent shopping bags.

"I think I should come with you today," he said anxiously, dismissing the formality of a greeting.

"Bruce, please," Ava said, sounding annoyed, waving him away with her hand. "Izzy, can you please explain to Bruce we can handle ourselves just fine?"

Bruce didn't respond but gave me a pleading look. I paused for a moment, "Bruce, we'll be calling on you for help, undoubtedly sooner than later. But right now the only place we're going is to the police station to see Mary and find out how she's holding up."

He sighed and looked at me, Jo, then Ava. "All right, but if you three go anywhere else after that, I'd like to know beforehand."

"Of course," I said, and Ava and Jo nodded adamantly in agreement.

He reluctantly acquiesced and watched us until we were out of sight, all the while folding his arms tightly across his chest.

The police station was small and basic. We saw Detective Jones as soon as we walked in the doors. He didn't look at all surprised to see us.

"Hello, ladies," he said, "I was expecting you."

"Detective Jones, how is Mary? Can we see her?" I requested.

"Mrs. Whitmore is in a holding cell waiting for her lawyer to arrive. She's declined to talk to us until he is with her. One of you, I repeat, *one* of you can go in and see her," he explained slowly.

"Thank you, sir," Jo said gratefully. "If we're quick, can we each take a turn to speak with her?"

Detective Jones nodded. "I don't see a problem with that, as long as you keep each visit short."

Jo went first. It gave Ava and me a chance to speak more with the detective.

"Sir, please, can you tell us why you arrested Mary so quickly? I mean have you considered any other suspects?" I asked.

"You jumped the gun a little bit is what she's saying," Ava quickly added.

"I just go where the facts take me, ladies," he stated.

"How can you arrest someone without any evidence?" Ava demanded.

"Listen, Mrs. Walsh and Mrs. Russell," Detective Jones began. "I didn't feel like I had to look any further because the evidence painted a clear picture."

I was silent as the memory of Mary's ring lying on the floor of the boathouse flashed before my eyes. Damn it.

"It looks like Mr. and Mrs. Whitmore were having some marital discord, even heading toward a split," the detective continued. "My guess is that after drinking too much wine, Mrs. Whitmore decided to give her husband a piece of her mind and things got out of hand. An argument turned physical and Mr. Whitmore ended up losing the fight."

Ava's looked surprised by how close the detective's knowledge was to yesterday's events leading up to the murder. Her tone shifted from indignant to desperate. "There is no way Mary did this."

I was puzzled. "Detective Jones, what makes you think the Whitmore's were getting a divorce?" I inquired, "Mary didn't mention any real problems between her and Charles until this morning. If they had a strained relationship, it certainly wasn't common knowledge."

"There was a lawyer's calling card sitting out on Mr. Whitmore's desk. Mr. Donald Henry, the name on the card, is a well-known divorce lawyer who specializes in scorned wives. We are well acquainted with him, as it is not uncommon for a domestic disturbance to occur when a couple decides to end their marriage. Perhaps Mrs. Whitmore taunted her husband with it, or maybe he found it among her things. Either way, it was probably the catalyst for a heated situation that ended in the most unfortunate of circumstances."

"While I respect your knowledge and experience in dealing with difficult and tumultuous relationships, Mary is just not a rash or violent person," I explained.

"Perhaps you don't understand me, Mrs. Walsh. I am not out to get Mrs. Whitmore. She has been polite to my officers and seems like a nice lady. But I have seen even the kindest of people change when love and pride turn into hate and humiliation." He said this with a somber insight of experience that made me shudder from thoughts of what this man must've seen in his lifetime.

I shook my head. "Detective Jones, Mary was only away from us for half an hour. If she had killed Charles, she wouldn't have been able to hide that something so terrible had happened. We have been the closest of friends for ten years. Please, do not close the book on this."

"Okay, look. I can already see the determination you three have to help your friend is going to end up with you meddling with my case. It's going to take some time to process the investigation and get the results of the autopsy, so I'll make you a deal: If you stay out of my way, I'll look deeper into other areas of Mr. Whitmore's life. But don't mistake my doing this as uncertainty. I am very confident the murderer is already behind bars." He looked at me and held out his hand.

I shook it. "Thank you so much for listening to us and not closing your mind. We will stay out of the investigation and let you do your job." I wondered if he knew I was lying when I made my promise.

Jo came back from her visit to Mary with tears in her eyes. I was next in line. Ava grabbed Jo's hand and sat down with her. Jo fell apart and Ava looked at me grimly.

An officer escorted me down a narrow hallway. Mary was sitting in a small cell. Her clothes were wrin-

kled and plain without their colorful accessories. I
guessed her scarf, belt, and earrings must've been confis-
cated upon arrest. Mary's mascara had also smudged, just
under her eyes, but the effect was pronounced, making
her look like she hadn't bathed in days. Even her posture
was noticeably altered, her usual tall, confident stance
replaced by drooping shoulders and a bowed head. She
rose up to greet me in spite of herself and tried to muster
a smile. Without her normal grooming and elegant styl-
ing, Mary was reduced to a much older, frail-looking ver-
sion of herself.

I gave her a big hug and we sat down next to each
other on a bench in the cell. I had a lot of questions that
needed answers but, first, I had to see what sort of state
she was in and how she was doing.

"How are you holding up?" I asked, feeling a little
awkward since the answer was quite obvious, but I needed to start somewhere.

Mary had tears in her eyes but she seemed determined not to let them fall. "I am a strong woman, Izzy,
but it's so hard to believe, so sudden. I'm grappling at the
idea of not being able to see, or even talk to, Charles
again. My situation here in jail is really not that bad, to be
honest. There is no place I could be that would comfort
me any more or any less."

"Is there anything I can do to help ease your loss?" I
asked.

"Nothing can take away that gnawing pain. It's almost easier that I don't have to face too many friends or family and show a brave face. I have time to be alone and nurture my sadness. It must sound crazy, but that's how I truly feel."

"That makes perfect sense to me," I replied, "But now I have to ask you to put aside your grief, just for a few minutes. We need to figure out who killed Charles. If we don't, you may spend the rest of your days in prison."

Mary looked at me and then nodded. "Okay," was the only response she seemed capable of vocalizing.

I squeezed her hand. "I need you to focus on what you saw the night Charles was killed, and who might have wanted him dead."

Mary sighed. "I've been so wrapped up in trying to come to terms with Charles's death, I've neglected to put much thought into my own situation."

"Did you see anything in the boathouse yesterday you didn't tell us about or that you may have over-looked?" I asked intently.

"I can't think of anything, really. I was so angry when I went in there I didn't notice much," she admitted.

"Anyone who may have been having problems with Charles? Maybe at work?"

Mary paused and began to look around the small cell. I felt like her attention was beginning to drift. I wondered if it was the first time she had taken notice of her surroundings.

"Um, he seemed to be busy so I don't think he had

any problems there—although he was considering parting
ways with William—"

I interrupted her thoughts. "That's a good start. Why
was he thinking of breaking ties with his partner?"

She didn't answer. She had become fixated on a
long, thin crack that went from floor to ceiling on the ad-
jacent cement wall. Although I was sitting beside her, I
felt like she had become distant.

"Mary?"

She jumped when I spoke. I was quite certain I
somehow startled her—as though she had forgotten I was
in the room. "Sorry, Izzy." She shut her eyes tightly for a
few seconds as if trying to refocus then continued to answer the question, "Charles and William hadn't been
close in many years but they had a strong working relationship. On top of that, the firm was doing really well.
So I was surprised to hear Charles talk of it. But I don't
think William even knew Charles was considering it. Unfortunately, with Charles and me not spending much time
together in recent days, I really didn't know much about
it. He told me rather casually so I'm not even sure if he
really meant it."

After she answered, she began to look distracted
again. I needed to press her for just a little longer. "What
else was going on in Charles's world?"

Mary hesitated. "I'm embarrassed to say I don't really know. When he wasn't working, he spent most of time
at the golf club, I suppose."

I was confused. "I thought you were involved with the club too."

"I was on the board of members for a long time but I left that position. I still go once or twice a month but I haven't been active with any club committees for quite a while."

"Why not?"

Mary slumped backward. She rubbed her eyes. "Does it matter?"

"That's what I need to find out. Please, Mary. I need you to focus for just a few more minutes."

She looked at me sadly, nodded, and then cast her eyes down. "Unfortunately, that's where Charles gained a reputation for being a flirt. Maggie Connors told me, in order to protect my dignity. I didn't want to see the truth. I still don't know the details of what actually happened. It could be nothing more than flirtations and gossip. It's not really important anymore, I suppose. But it was bad enough to make Maggie bring it to my attention. I quit the board after she told me."

How humiliating, I thought. Mary was a proud woman. It must have been awful to find out her husband had behaved so despicably, especially in a place where she was so involved. I said nothing but looked at her sympathetically.

She smiled wistfully, the tears now streaming down her face. "As I explained to you all yesterday, I have lived with his philandering for a long time. Even after I

found out, I made excuses for him. I had myself convinced it was my own fault for marrying such a charming
man. I thought, no matter what woman he carried on
with, he only loved me and that was enough. What a fool
I was."

Although under different circumstances, I knew what
humiliation felt like. "Don't be so hard on yourself. You
loved him and wanted your marriage to work. It takes
many of us a little longer than we'd like to admit when
something is not working. Remember when I thought I
could become a professional artist? My painting skills
were mediocre at best but I had myself convinced I had a
unique style."

Mary giggled, in spite of herself. "Well, they were
one of a kind, and very colorful. I still have one in my
library."

"Yes, because you're a loyal friend. My point is that
I didn't want to face the truth. It took almost two years of
lessons and effort to finally recognize that it would never
be more than a hobby. No matter how much I wanted to
paint like Emily Carr, it wasn't going to happen. You
were in the process of accepting the truth and looking at
your options: seeing a lawyer—whether or not you were
planning to go through with it—was a big step. I think
confronting Charles was really a way of putting your own
feet to the fire and moving on with it."

Mary seemed to be feeling a little better—she had
started to look me in the eye again. "Maybe. Just going to

see that lawyer and recognizing that I had some rights and some choices made me feel better than I had in a long time."

"Mary, we need to figure this out so you can heal. Not just from Charles's death but from years of a complicated and painful marriage. You have our support and willingness to help but you need to help us. I want you to think about who could have killed him. We can start with his partner but there may be others. If Charles was carrying on with married women, I can imagine there are some angry husbands out there. Perhaps a few jilted women, too. It's not going to be easy to think about. But I need you to be strong. I have to be able to ask personal questions."

Mary took a moment then sat up confidently. Something in our talk must've connected with her; revived her wounded spirit. "Darling, you're right. I can be as strong as anyone. I'm not going to sit here and wallow. I did not kill Charles, and whoever did needs to be brought to justice—for me, and for poor Charles. He may have been a lousy husband but he certainly didn't deserve that end."

It was a huge relief to see Mary rise above her self-doubt and pain. "I'm glad to hear you say that, Mary. Now, can you give me any suggestions about where we should begin looking?"

I could see she was already starting to think with more clarity because her eyes began to focus more now. She stood up tall and began to pace about the confined area. Finally, she looked at me intently, nodding enthusiastically. "The club. I would definitely go there first. Gossip spreads like wild fire. And in a place full of people with lots of money, time, and privilege, there's a lot to go around. I'll admit I used to really enjoy it too, until, of course, I realized my husband was one of the juiciest topics."

I scrunched up my nose. "Yes, I could see how that could dampen the fun."

The door opened to the holding area and an officer told me my time was up. I gave Mary a hug and assured her she wouldn't be there long. She seemed better, and stronger, than she had just a few minutes before. Mary's lawyer arrived as I emerged from my visit so Ava, Jo, and I left the police station. My head was swirling with ideas. I was anxious to talk them through with my friends and come up with our plan.

"Where to?" Jo asked as we got into the car.

I revved the engine. "Let's go to my place and figure out our next move. There's no time to waste."

"Good idea," Ava said. "My house gets loud and there will be too many interruptions to talk properly. Plus, Bruce will hover."

"Mine should be empty," I told them. "Frank was going to take the kids out for a while to give me a little space."

Jo, who was sitting in the back seat, leaned forward to make sure she didn't miss a word. "He's not at work?"

"No, he got his assistant in to work at the shop today. He loves having an excuse to take the kids out. He gets to eat ice cream and run around in the sunshine, two of his favorite things," I explained.

Ava pulled her sunglasses out of her purse and put them on determinedly. She pointed dead ahead. "Let's burn rubber."

Chapter 13

I was wrong about having an empty house. The kids were still outside and Frank was pretending to be reading. I could tell by the look of concern in his face that he had been waiting for me to get home. We filled him in on what we knew. The worry in his eyes remained. I suspected that, until all this was sorted out, I'd be seeing that expression on a daily basis.

He also had a few questions. "So, what is it that you three plan to do to help Mary? I'd like to think that you will stick to bringing her some magazines and toiletries so she's more comfortable while she's detained."

I hadn't exactly detailed our intention so I sensed he was fishing for information. "That's a thoughtful idea, Frank."

Ava patted Frank's shoulder. "Yes, reading the latest advice on how to prepare a roast would give any woman comfort, Frank."

Luckily, Frank knew Ava well enough to let her snarky comment roll off his shoulders. "My point is you should listen to the detective. All three of you need to remember that there's a killer on the loose. You're not dealing with some Nancy Drew type of mystery here. Any person who can look someone in the eye and proceed to kill that person is not someone to be trifled with. If someone was willing to kill Charles in cold blood, they will not hesitate to turn and kill any or all of you next."

He had a point. "Frank, you know we'll be careful and not put ourselves in harm's way."

His eyes flashed in a rare show of anger. I guessed he was growing increasingly frustrated at our dismissive attitude. "You don't even know the person you're dealing with here. How can you be careful if you don't even know who you can trust?" he demanded.

Jo turned to him. "Frank, we know we can trust each other. We will cap it there, promise."

"Honey, we're not setting out to look for trouble," I explained. "We're doing what we are compelled to do: help our friend. There's no way any of us can sit by and wait. It's not in our nature."

I could see he was beginning to calm down, or at least listening to our reasoning and logic. He ran his hand through his hair. "I understand your need to help your friend, I do. I want to help in any way I can, too. But you must remember how dangerous this could become," he argued in a final plea to be careful.

"I know I'll be hearing these same words when I get home, too. We will stick together and keep you and Bruce informed of each and every move," Ava promised.

"I'm going to hold you to that—*all three of you*. I mean it," Frank warned.

Ava saluted him. "Yes, sir."

"Honey, I promise, too. Now can you please take the kids out so we can have some time to talk?" I asked lightly.

He agreed, albeit grudgingly. He went to find the kids and plan their day. I made some more coffee. Ava, Jo, and I sat down.

Jo cleared her throat. "Okay, girls, where do we start?"

They were both looking at me.

Ava raised her eyebrows and looked at me expectantly. "Izzy, you spent the most time talking to Mary at the police station so I think we're both assuming you have some ideas."

"I do," I said confidently.

She smoothed back her hair slowly. "That's a relief. My head is still spinning from what's happened in the last day, or is it two days. I'm so confused right now I'll just stop talking—but I am listening," she added with a slight smile.

I grabbed a pad of paper and a pencil from a nearby drawer. "It has been a crazy few days and, because of that, I think we should go over some of the facts. What do we know? What do we need to find out? Who comes up on the short list of suspects?"

Jo scratched her head. "Should I be writing this down, too?"

Ava smiled. "Girls, at this point I don't think we know enough to write anything down!"

I disagreed. "I think we know more than we've given ourselves credit for. We're the ones who found Charles. That's a big start."

Ava raised her hands. "You may be right but, other than seeing Charles on the floor covered in blood, I don't remember much."

Jo looked at her. "Have you tried to remember it with your eyes closed?"

Ava shook her head and gave it a try. I followed suit.

I tried to scan the room using my memory. As the scene slowly unfolded in my mind, there were details I remembered and black spots where I didn't.

I slapped the table and opened my eyes. "I just remembered something. What about the two empty wine glasses and unopened bottle of wine? Considering it was still sitting there in melting ice, I have to assume it wasn't just for decoration."

Ava's eyes flashed. "Oh geez, you're right. And it couldn't have been Mary he was waiting for. Not only was she entertaining us, they had had that terrible fight. I couldn't see him trying to break out the romance so soon after."

I nodded. "Exactly,"

"Are you two suggesting that Charles was entertaining a woman when he was killed?" Jo asked.

Ava tapped her finger on her lips. "No man is going to chill a bottle of wine for another man—beer maybe, but not a cool Chardonnay. I think we're really onto something."

I opened the notebook I had yet to write in, with the pen poised. "Let's not get ahead of ourselves. If Charles had a female visitor, what could that mean?"

Ava pounded her fist on the table. "The scoundrel was finally taken down by one of his floozies."

Jo shook her head. "I would find it hard to imagine a woman being able to overpower Charles. He was very fit."

Ava raised an eyebrow. "Don't underestimate the power of surprise, my dear."

"I agree with you both. I think it's a possibility but we need to consider others, too," I urged.

Ava snapped her fingers. "What if Charles were expecting a woman but a jealous husband or boyfriend showed up instead?"

Jo rubbed her forehead. "Good point, I hadn't thought of that."

"Charles didn't seem to have much respect for the

institution of marriage. I bet we could find some pretty angry husbands out there," Ava noted.

I put the pen down for a moment. "It's possible but Mary isn't certain his indiscretions went beyond immature flirtations with anyone."

Ava hesitated. "True, but it was enough to create nasty rumors around the golf club."

"You're right," I conceded.

Jo reached over and grabbed the notebook and pen. "You two are skipping ahead. We need to stay on point. Let's get back to the crime scene. You guys think and I'll write."

I rubbed my temples. "Okay."

"Spoken like a pro," Ava remarked.

I closed my eyes again and began to bite my nails. "There was some papers scattered on the desk. Next to them, was another bottle of booze but I can't remember what it was."

"It was Whiskey—maybe Scotch?" Ava asked.

I opened my eyes to look at her. Her eyes were now shut. I could tell she was concentrating because the few forehead wrinkles she had were showing. It was a rare display. "There was glass shattered across the floor. No, wait, it must've been crystal—Waterford Crystal if I had to guess—nothing sparkles like that stuff. It even shone through…"

Ava opened her eyes in a flash and looked at me, not able to look away. She must've realized the significance of her recollection, as I just had. I fell back in my seat and my eyes were wide open and she covered her cheeks to try and hide the rosy flush that had suddenly come up.

Jo looked from her to me. "What am I missing?"

I broke Ava's gaze and turned to Jo. "A few weeks ago Mary splurged on some Waterford Crystal snifters for Charles. Charles was probably drinking whisky from one when he was killed."

Ava regained her composure. "That would explain the strong smell and the shattered glass—I mean crystal."

"So what?" Jo demanded.

"So, my dear, Charles was probably holding a drink when he was killed," Ava said.

Jo gasped. "I get it. He didn't realize he was in danger."

"Exactly," I asserted, "It suggests that Charles might've been killed by someone he trusted—or at least someone he didn't consider a physical threat."

"Right," Jo added. "If he had been worried, he would've put his drink down and prepared to defend himself."

I nodded to indicate she understood.

Jo was about to write something down. Then she tossed the notebook aside in a display of impatience and put her elbow and the table. She propped her chin forward. "So, who is on the short list of suspects?"

I remembered Mary had mentioned some possible changes with his career. "Mary told me there might've been some trouble between Charles and his partner, William Stormwell."

"Enough for a motive?" Ava asked.

"Mary said Charles might've been leaving the firm."

Ava raised her eyebrows. "That could do it. Money and power are two biggies."

Jo held up her hand. "Are you sure? Didn't they go to college together?"

"Maybe, but it doesn't sound like they spent much time together socially," I said. "That brings up another question: whether they liked each other or not, why part ways if they had a successful business and partnership?"

"Good point," Jo said.

"Maybe William is simply a decent man and didn't want a letch of a partner anymore," Ava commented.

I sighed, feeling slightly annoyed. "Ava, the man is dead. Do you really need to go on calling him names?"

"Listen, girls," Ava said. "The way I see it, people who stay out of trouble rarely end up murdered in their own home. The more we find out about the dearly departed Charles, the more I'm surprised he lasted so long!"

She had a point, as crude as it was. If Charles hadn't been behaving in such a careless way, perhaps he wouldn't have met such a violent end.

"What's our next step?" Jo asked.

I looked at her. "It depends. You're still going to be staying at the Whitmore's house, right?"

Jo shrugged. "I have a week of vacation and Mary

wanted me to stay at her place before all of this happened. I hadn't really thought about it since, but if it
helps, I'll definitely keep those plans."

"Yes, I think it might," I proposed. "It'll give us day
and night access to the house which could provide some
good insight. I think we should talk to Mrs. Collins again
and find out her thoughts on all this."

Jo nodded in agreement. "Sounds good."

I turned to Ava. "Why don't you and Jo start there?"
I suggested. "I'll drop you off. Mrs. Collins is the only
person who's been at the house full-time, aside from
Mary and Charles, for years. She probably knows what
Charles was up to as much as Mary does, perhaps even
more."

"What about you?" Ava demanded.

I stood up. "I'm going to stop by and talk to Mary
again, if the police let me. I have thought of a few more
questions I need to ask her. She mentioned that Charles
spent a lot of time at the golf club. I want to head over
there afterward. We need to find out if he was rubbing
anyone the wrong way."

Ava got up and stretched her long arms over her
head. "Or if he was rubbing anyone the *right* way," she
added dryly.

I slapped her arms down. "Yes, to put it crassly. I
want to get there before the police do."

Ava frowned at me. "If they get there, you mean.
They might've settled on Mary being the one and only
suspect."

I doubted it. "Detective Jones struck me as a smart and thorough investigator. Even if he felt strongly that Mary was guilty, it would be irresponsible not to sort through the rest of Charles's life to find out everything he could."

Jo was the first one to the door. She looked anxious. "Let's get moving."

I ran to the backyard and bid my family a hasty good-bye, promising to call Frank later. I was quite certain he would've had more to say if the kids were not in earshot. I ran away before he had a chance.

I grabbed my keys on the way out. "Okay girls, I'm all set."

I made sure not to look in the rearview mirror in case Frank had come out the front to talk privately. I wasn't ready to make any concrete assurances to him other than a generic promise to stay safe. The three of us would not rest until Mary was freed and the real killer was found. What that meant and where it would lead us, I really didn't know.

Chapter 14

I dropped off Ava and Jo at Mary's with a promise to call them later so we could exchange information. Then I drove back to the police station where I almost walked right into Detective Jones. He was on his way out when I was coming in.

"Mrs. Walsh, I have a hunch I better get used to seeing you a lot over the coming days," he remarked.

"Yes, Detective Jones, I'm planning to be here as much as I can and as much as you'll let me. Mary needs my support."

"I understand that. How about I make you a deal: You stay out of my way and I'll try to give you some extra time with your friend."

"Thank you, sir. That sounds like a fair deal to me."

He looked at me intently. "You understand that means you stay out of the police investigation, right?"

It occurred to me that he asked me the same question earlier today. "Yes, sir, I will. I promise," I looked him in the eye and meant it. After all, I wasn't getting involved in the police investigation; I had my own to focus on!

Detective Jones escorted me back inside and instructed an officer to allow me fifteen minutes with Mary. She was sitting quietly in the cell and stood up when I walked in. Her face lit up and she smiled.

"Back already? You know I'm fine in here. You don't need to come and check in on me every spare second you have," she scolded me. "Of course, I can't deny I'm happy to see you again."

I hugged her. It gave me a small sense of relief since she wasn't shaky anymore; she felt stronger. "I'm not here to check up on you. This time I need your help."

She sat down and made sure there was enough room for me to sit next to her. "What can I do?"

I joined her on the small bench. "I wanted to make sure Maggie Connors is a trusted friend at the golf club."

"You met her. What you see is what you get. Honest, kind, and trustworthy. Why?" Mary inquired.

"I want her to show me around the club and introduce me to some of the members. I'm guessing no one there knows about what's happened yet. I'd like to find out if there's anyone at the club that Charles was having problems with. I'll head over to his office tomorrow but since it's closed today I thought I'd take the opportunity to go to the club first."

Mary raised her eyebrows. "Well, it's the best day to be there if you want to see the most people, I suppose. They have a weekly brunch that is very popular, plus it's the busiest day on the course."

"I assume the brunch would bring as many women as there is men to the club?"

Mary nodded. "Definitely. It's usually when everyone gets together and relaxes, discussing the weeks' events and happenings. It's a fairly tight-knit little community."

"Good, that's just what I was hoping."

Mary cocked her head to the side and looked at me. "What are you expecting to find?"

I met her eyes. "I'm not really sure, but I have a hunch I'll find something, if that makes any sense."

"Nothing makes sense to me right now, to be honest. However, Maggie will be a good guide to the club. She knows just about everyone and everything going on there," Mary explained, "Her husband, Harold, is—sorry, was—a good friend of Charles."

"Yes, I think she mentioned that. Okay, great. I've got to run, Mary, I'm sorry."

She squeezed my arm. "It's all right. Just be careful."

I faltered getting up. "I'll be back very soon, I promise."

"Go, Izzy. It's not like you can take me with you," she instructed, seeing my hesitancy.

Once I left Mary's cell, my hesitation vanished. I walked with purpose out the police station and drove straight home. I was relieved to find Frank and the children finally out. I called Maggie immediately. The phone rang so many times I had almost given up when a faint voice finally answered.

"Maggie? Hi, it's Isabelle Walsh."

"Isabelle," I could hear her voice cracking, "The police were just here and told me about Charles."

"That's why I'm calling. I was hoping to come and see you right away."

"Of course," she said, "Come on over."

Maggie gave me the directions to her home and I hopped in the car. Ten minutes later, I parked in front of her house. I was in no way surprised to find it almost as beautiful as Mary's. It was a solid brick home with a large front lawn. Colorful flowers were blooming in an extensive garden that ran along the front of the house under the windows. It, too, was an oceanfront property not far from the center of town.

Maggie greeted me at the door. She was wearing a long, full skirt with a pink blouse tucked in. She smiled warmly through red, puffy eyes and welcomed me into her home. Tea and biscuits were set on a table in a bright, open sitting room.

I gave her a quick hug. "Thank you for seeing me so soon."

"I'm glad you're here, Isabelle. Please, come in," she led me to the room with the snacks.

"How are you holding up?" I asked. My question seemed to initiate a new wave of emotion. It took Maggie a minute to compose herself before she could answer. I regretted my question.

I momentarily wondered if I was either unfeeling or still in shock. My only thoughts since Charles's death were after the welfare of Mary. I hadn't thought much about the principal victim. Then a little voice popped into my head. It sounded an awful lot like Ava. *Don't kid yourself, Izzy. You never cared for the man when he was alive, why would you give a damn now?* I chased the obnoxious voice out of my head and looked from side to side inconspicuously to make sure Ava wasn't actually in the room.

Luckily, Maggie didn't notice. She finally managed to get her words out. "I'm just stunned and overwhelmed with sadness, as I'm sure everyone else is—in particular Mary."

I pressed my lips together firmly. It forced my dimple to show—a trick I used as a teenager to try and feign sorrow and regret the few times I was caught for a misdeed. "Yes, of course."

Maggie seemed to buy my expression. I kept it up as she went on. "As you know, Mary has been a good friend for many years. I'd like to be there to help in any way I can. I am very much in the dark about what's happened. All I know is that Charles was killed. The police wouldn't give me any more information and I can't seem to get a hold of Mary. They came by to talk to my husband, I assume because he and Charles were very close. But he had left for the golf club already."

I saw no way to sugarcoat the facts. "Mary can't call you because she's been arrested for murder."

She blinked a few times as her face drained of color. "I don't understand."

I filled her in with what I knew. It took a few minutes for her to get over the shock. But I needed to press on with the reason I was there.

"Maggie, I've got to find out more about Charles's life at the golf club. I need to know what people thought of him and if he had been having problems with any other members."

She looked at me blankly and then sat down. Her eyes closed and her hands reached up and began to methodically rub her temples in a circular motion. I didn't interrupt what I guessed was an automatic reaction to stress. I just sat quietly across from her and waited. When she looked up at me a moment later she seemed more coherent.

"Sorry, Isabelle, I just needed a moment there."

"Please don't apologize, Maggie. It's a shocking and terrible situation. I'm sorry to be the one to tell you about Mary's arrest."

"Is that why you're here?" she inquired.

"Yes, it is. I'm hoping you can tell me more about his social life. Mary believes he spent most of his free time at the golf club. It sounds like he may have created some ripples. I thought maybe you could fill me in."

Maggie seemed to consider my request carefully before answering. "Charles was well liked, Isabelle. As I'm sure you know, he was charming and funny. That made him very popular, overall. He was also very friendly. Everyone knew him and it was rare to hear any sort of negative words spoken about him. The news will be felt deeply in the club, I'm sure." She paused. "I must apologize. I'm still finding this whole thing very hard to believe."

"I agree. I'm trying to stay focused on finding out the truth and hope that it will help me deal with what happened," I confessed.

Maggie seemed to understand. She smiled at me sympathetically through strained eyes.

"Was there anyone Charles recently had problems with?" I asked.

"Come to think of it, there was an incident a few weeks ago that apparently got a little heated out on the golf course. My understanding is there were some strong words exchanged between Charles and another man, Donald Wright. I don't know the details but I believe Charles was teasing Donald. He got fed up and became angry," Maggie explained.

I was no expert on the game or its conduct and etiquette. "Is it that unusual for men to exchange words during a game?"

Here eyes locked with mine. "It is when they're not playing each other."

I didn't need to be a golf ace to recognize that sort of tension. My heart skipped a beat. "Do you know what the exchange was about?"

"Not exactly, but it wasn't the first argument they've had. There was certainly no love lost between the two."

"Why is that?" I probed.

Maggie hesitated before saying, "I try to avoid spreading rumors and listening to gossip, however, in light of what's happened I will tell you. There are some people who believe that Charles may have spent too much time with Donald's wife, Sharon, a few months ago."

"Are you suggesting they had an affair?" I asked directly.

Maggie squirmed in her seat uncomfortably. "I don't know. That's just what I've heard in whispers here and there. My understanding is that Donald grew suspicious but Sharon and Charles both denied any wrongdoing."

"Did *you* ever notice Charles and Sharon spending time together?" I pressed.

"I did, but they were working on a fundraiser together so it may have been quite innocent."

"The way you say that makes me doubt you thought it was innocent," I observed.

Maggie sighed. "I did notice there was an awful lot of giggles and whispering exchanged between the two. I haven't seen anyone quite so enraptured planning a fund-raiser before. However, nothing ever seemed to come of it. In fact, Charles and Sharon practically acted like strangers after that."

I bit my lip. "Was it just the displays of silly talk that made you wonder?"

"Not really, no. What struck me as odd was the intense distrust and dislike Donald sustained for Charles. The altercation on the golf course was not an isolated incident. They seemed to have run-ins fairly often."

"That could be very important, Maggie." I stated, "Were there more rumors involving Charles and other women, as well?"

"I'm afraid so. A while back, the club's former pastry chef, Betty Smith, was caught in some sort of compromising position with Charles and was let go immediately," Maggie informed me.

"Do you know what happened to her after she left?"

"No idea. She just seemed to disappear. If I knew where she was working, I would've gone to buy some of her flans and tarts. They were the best I've ever had, but probably wouldn't be well received, being a club member," Maggie admitted.

"Why not?"

"Miss Smith wasn't happy about being let go. She said Charles was a creep. But Charles said *she* was the one making advances and the board members sided with him. Rumor has it she felt humiliated and left the club a very angry young woman," she said.

"Hmm, that's very interesting. Have you heard of any other women complaining about unwelcome advances by Charles?" I wondered.

"Not at all," she assured me.

"Okay, that's good to know."

"I should warn you Mary is not aware of any of this. I confessed to her there was talk surrounding Charles but luckily she picked up on what I couldn't quite say so she never asked about the details. No one ever told her, as far as I know," Maggie explained.

"You're a good friend," I observed.

"So is Mary. Can she have visitors? I'd like to go see her now if I can," she hoped.

"Before you do, would you mind taking me to the club and introducing me to a few people? I want to talk to some of the members before the police do."

"Not a problem," Maggie said, "Do you want to let people know about Charles's passing? I'm sure no one there is aware of it yet."

"Just the opposite, actually," I noted.

She looked confused. "I don't understand."

"I want to get there before people find out. I need to get their true opinions of Charles. I think when someone dies people tend to alter their thoughts about them, often without even meaning to do it. It's much easier to be critical of someone when they're above ground."

"You know, I think you're right. I wonder why that is," Maggie pondered.

"My guess is that most people do it out of respect for

the dead." I paused, "Although I wouldn't be surprised if a few people are scared they're being watched by the dead soul."

"Do you think that's why?" Maggie whispered.

I sensed I was beginning to add to Maggie's stress. I needed to be more careful about what I said. "Regardless of the reasons, it'll be much more difficult to obtain any dirt about Charles if the news gets out before I have a few questions answered. The fact that Charles was murdered may soften even the harshest of critic's opinions."

"I suppose that's true," Maggie agreed. "Let's get over there then. I know just who you need to meet."

"Excellent. Who is it?" I asked.

"Jane Humphries, the queen bee of gossip," Maggie stated, "Nothing escapes her radar."

"Sounds a little intimidating," I admitted.

Maggie's hunched shoulders began to relax as the conversation focused on the club. "Jane can be a bit of a bully. She has somewhat of a monopoly on the newsreel around the club. Everyone knows it's important to stay in her good books. She can make life around there quite difficult for anyone she doesn't like. Think of her like a newspaper editor: she can focus attention on stories she wants heard and away from those she doesn't. And remember: there's no impartiality when it comes to reporting. She has a way of angling a story to make someone look quite innocent or downright immoral."

"Interesting," I noted.

"We better get there soon or we'll miss some of the people you'll probably want to meet," Maggie informed me.

"It's only ten o'clock in the morning," I observed.

"You mean it's *already* ten o'clock in the morning. Tee off starts as early as five-thirty or six a.m. for some," Maggie explained.

My mouth fell open. "Isn't it still dark then?"

"A little, but some people love to be on the course at the break of dawn. Charles was one of those dedicated golfers."

I was confounded "What on earth for?"

"There are a few reasons, actually. First, it's quiet and peaceful. Second, the weather is much more tolerable. There's no need to worry about overheating or sunstroke. And, finally, some of the members just love to be the first ones to use the tee. It gives them the nicest grass to start their game on."

"Geez, this is a whole world I'm not familiar with. Good thing I have you as a guide," I said gratefully.

We headed out in separate cars, since Maggie was going to see Mary afterward. The parking lot was almost full by the time we got there. When we entered the club, there was a buzz and a vitality that I didn't really expect. I always thought of golf as a subdued, quiet activity. But folks here were full of energy. People were smiling, loudly calling out to one another across the room, and engaged in lively conversations. I guessed rising with the sun and getting that fresh morning air and activity really agreed with people. I was still taking in the scene when Maggie grabbed my arm.

She led me over to a tall, very thin, blonde woman with a blinding white outfit. The lady looked like she was getting ready to play. "Jane, before you tee off I'd like to introduce you to Isabelle Walsh, a friend of Mary Whitmore's."

Jane's beady eyes seemed able look me up and down faster than I could open my mouth. She gave me a disparaging smile. "Hello Isabelle. Pleased to meet you."

I instantly wished I had ironed my blouse. "Nice to meet you, too, Jane."

Maggie touched my elbow. "Isabelle, this is the exceptional Jane Humphries I told you about. Jane is our social convener and knows just about everyone at this club." She then excused herself to go get a cup of coffee.

As soon as Maggie walked away, I turned to Jane. "It's a beautiful club you've got here."

"Thank you, Isabelle. Now, I hope you've brought something else to change into if you intend to play," Jane advised as she glanced at my outfit contemptuously. "There is a strict dress code on the course."

"Oh, yes, of course. But I'm not here to play. Maggie and Mary told me they served the best brunch in town so I had to come by and find out for myself."

"Make sure you get the eggs benedict. It beats any item on the menu," Jane instructed, "Now where is

Mary? I haven't seen her around this morning."

"I'm meeting her here soon. She's probably just running behind," I lied.

She looked at me keenly. "That's good to hear. She hasn't been around much. I thought that perhaps the silly rumors floating around scared her off. I'm glad she's paying as little attention to them as I am."

I matched her look. "I'm sorry, rumors? I don't know what you mean."

She flipped her hair over her shoulder and looked bored. "Oh, you know, Isabelle, any place people gather, people talk. I'm sure it's nothing."

"Rumors about Mary?" I pressed.

Her beady eyes now met mine. She knew she had me hooked. "Not about Mary, of course, but that naughty little husband of hers. He always seems to get people talking."

"Talking about what?"

Jane surveyed the room then leaned in to me. "If you know Mary, you must know Charles. He and his...*outgoing* personality just seem to get him into trouble. This month it was with Donald Wright, a while before that, it was more of a staffing issue. Don't make me expand, Isabelle. I am not one to gossip."

I thought this might be a good opportunity to stir the pot a little. "Mary mentioned there was a little trouble with some overbearing husband. She said the gentleman totally overreacted."

Jane looked surprised. "Well, we all know Charles is a harmless flirt." She hesitated. "*However,* Sharon and Charles did spend an awful lot of time together, more than my husband would like *me* to spend with another man, I'd venture to say. Donald really did take it to heart, though. After a bit of a run-in between the two men last week, I actually heard Donald say one day Charles was going to push him too far and he'd regret it. It gave me chills to see Donald so angry."

"Wow, that's quite a threat. Do you think he'd ever try and hurt Charles?" I inquired with wide eyes.

"Don't worry, darling. I'm sure it was just his ego talking. It may not sound like it, but Donald is normally a very mild-mannered man. Charles just knew he could get under Donald's skin and I think it amused him. It certainly garnered an audience whenever the two were together."

I leaned in even closer to the queen bee. "I'm intrigued. Mary made light of the whole thing. What about Donald's wife, Sharon?"

"To be honest, no one really noticed Sharon before Charles took an interest in her. And now that she pretends not to see him whenever they're near one another, I'm afraid she once again mostly slips under the radar. Sharon is a rather meek, younger woman who mostly keeps to her self. She can be found usually reading a book by the window while Donald is out on the course." She paused then pointed not so subtly across the room. "I spot her right now. She is the mildly attractive blonde sitting in the big chair over there with her nose deep inside that magazine."

"Small world," I commented.

"It is around here, Isabelle. Now, I think I've shared more of my fair share of gossip for the day, so you just tell Mary that she absolutely must come and find me before she leaves so we can set up a brunch date next week," Jane ordered.

"I will," I answered automatically.

Jane excused herself and I watched her float off to a group of ladies and begin asking if they had heard the latest "news" about some other unsuspecting club member. I knew just the person I needed to talk to next. She was intently focused on what she was reading, or at least appeared to be.

As I approached Sharon Wright, I giggled to myself as Jane's description of this woman repeated in my mind. Calling Mrs. Wright a "mildly attractive" woman was outright laughable. She could only be accurately described as a knockout. She might be as quiet as Jane said, but there was no way that the leggy blonde sitting by the window could've gone unnoticed. Her looks were the type normally reserved for the silver screen.

I did a leap in the air—strictly in my imagination— as I saw what she was reading because I recognized the magazine and, in turn, an opportunity. I knew exactly how to start this conversation.

"Excuse me," I began.

Mrs. Wright looked up, a little surprised. "Yes?"

"Is that *Enchanted* magazine?" I inquired.

"Yes—it is," she said, a little hesitantly.

I smiled. "When I saw you with it, I couldn't help but come over. It looks a little different from the one I read."

Sharon paused and looked me over and a shy grin appeared on her flawless face. "It's the French edition," she gushed, "My cousin sends it from France every month. The articles are often similar but the fashion is worlds better."

"I didn't even know there was a French edition. I'm not very adventurous in my own style but I love seeing the couture collections. I like to daydream that my life may one day require me to choose a dress they showcase," I admitted.

"Some of the French designers make the rest of the fashion world look like a group of amateurs," she whispered.

"I won't argue with that," I said. "My name is Isabelle, by the way."

"Pardon me, I'm Sharon." She paused. "I don't think I've seen you here before."

"I'm just here as a guest. Although, if you always read those magazines with the focus I saw today, I'm surprised you ever notice anyone," I teased.

She covered her face with the magazine and then

peeked out from behind it, playfully. "I'll admit I can get pretty absorbed. Besides, I'm not really much for big social gatherings."

"Are you French?" I inquired.

"My parents are French so I grew up with it. Reading books and magazines help keep up my language skills. At least that's what I tell my husband," she confessed.

"I just met another French woman, who also really adores fashion. Isn't that a coincidence?" I asked, thinking of how stylish Erica Dorner was at Mary's.

"I must tell you, I think many of us share that passion," she confessed.

"I have a feeling she'll be green with envy when I tell her about seeing your magazine," I said .

"You must take it for her. I'm a little embarrassed to tell you this is the third time I've read it."

I hesitated. "Are you sure?"

She smiled genuinely. "Absolutely. As soon as my husband arrives, I'll give it to you. You'll make her day, I promise."

I was touched. "That is very kind. Thank you."

"You're welcome, Isabelle. The next issue will be arriving in two weeks, anyways, and I have a library book sitting at home waiting for me to open it."

Sharon became distracted by a small group of boisterous men entering the club. The foursome had clearly just finished an enjoyable round of golf, their cheeks rosy and their spirits high. I could see on Sharon's face she

was disappointed. It clearly wasn't the person she was
hoping to see.

"Are you a golfer, too?" I asked, trying to keep our
conversation going.

She shook her head. "My husband loves golf but it's
not really my sport. He plays, I read, and together we
dine."

"He must've teed off early," I commented.

She peeked her head over the chair to look at the entrance once again. "Actually, he's not even here yet."

Now I understood why Sharon had been so interested
in the group of men who just passed. I looked at her curiously, waiting for her to expand.

"Oh, sorry, we have a sailboat docked at Twin Oaks
Harbor," she explained. "During the summer months,
Donald will often spend the night. He finds it relaxing in
the heat of the summer. I'm not as much of a boat enthu-
siast so I'm quite happy to stay home on solid ground."

"Sounds like a pretty good arrangement," I said.

"It's not a life of couture dresses, but it works for us.
Besides, he named his boat the *Sharon's Beauty*. Donald
tells me he's spending the night with my nautical entity
so it's like he's with me in spirit. I'm happy with the sentiment," she joked. "Although, I'm wondering if he forgot about the *real* me as he's almost half an hour late for
our brunch date," she added, looking around again.

My interest was piqued. "Is he usually late when he
meets you after sleeping on the boat? If my husband and I

had that arrangement, I probably wouldn't see him before noon."

"Donald's normally quite punctual. It's no big deal. I'm quite content sitting here," she said casually.

"My husband could use a little reminder about consideration, too, sometimes," I lied. "It would be nice if there was some sort of gentleman training before marriage, wouldn't it?"

"I suppose," she answered. I could see she was losing interest in our little chat. I tried to sound casual when I asked her, "With Donald so busy with his hobbies do you ever get lonely? I'm sure you have no shortage of male attention."

She eyed me apprehensively. "Donald is a wonderful, loving husband. As a happily married woman, I have no need for anyone else's attention."

Dammit, I thought. Clearly, I had hit a nerve. I blushed, stammering, "S—Sharon, I didn't mean to suggest otherwise."

It was too late. Her guard was up. "You never mentioned who your friends were at the club."

Before I could say anything in response, the loud speaker crackled overhead, saving me from answering her question.

"Good morning, members and guests. Could we please have everyone's attention as we have some sad news to share with all of you? We have just found out we've lost one of our members. It is with a heavy heart we must inform you that Charles Whitmore passed away over the weekend. We would like to extend our condolences to his family and friends here at the club. We have no further details to impart at this time. Thank you for your attention."

I watched Sharon as the announcement of Charles's death was read, and I noticed her complexion change from light and glowing to heavy and ashen. She looked up at me momentarily then back down at the floor. She scrambled out of her seat, the magazine dropping from her lap to the floor. While I had hoped to be here before club members found out about Charles, I now realized watching Sharon's reaction, being here *as* they found out could prove to be even more telling.

"E—Excuse me, Isabelle," she muttered, almost tripping on her words. "It's been nice talking with you but I forgot there is somewhere I was supposed to be."

I caught her eye. "Sharon, are you all right?"

"Yes, I'm fine, thank you," she answered mechanically and, with that, she practically ran out of the club. I picked up her magazine and put it in my purse. Something struck me as I watched her go. There was an expression written all over her face, and I could only use one word to describe it: fear.

I looked around the rest of the room and saw that Sharon wasn't the only one with a strong reaction, even though no one else looked nearly as scared. Charles's death had sent a shockwave throughout the club. It was almost silent for a few seconds as everyone absorbed the news. The only sound was that of Sharon's high heel shoes clicking as she ran, with virtually everyone in the room watching her leave. Following her exit, a loud uproar of excited conversation and emotional outbursts began as people began to discuss the news of Charles's passing.

I made my way back over to the gossip queen, Jane Humphries. She was talking to a small group of ladies who were hanging on her every word.

As I approached her, she was in the middle of a sentence. "...his complexion was so pallid and I said to him he just wasn't looking well. The poor man should've listened to me. He might still be alive if he had just taken a little bit of friendly advice—" She stopped talking when she saw me and dramatically rushed to my side. "You poor darling. Now you know why Mary is late meeting you this morning. Our friend must be reeling over the sudden death of her beloved."

I smiled at her awkwardly and hastily replied, "Yes, of course."

Jane's beady eyes ambushed mine with a burrowing gaze. I was certain she was trying to read my mind. "Now, I hope you're not too upset by that hussy Sharon Wright rushing out the door, obviously saddened by the death of her flirtatious friend. How tacky of her to have to draw attention to herself in the face of such a loss."

A jolt of sympathy for Sharon struck me. "Charles's

death is shocking news. It's always hard to judge how anyone is going to react, I suppose." Good thing the blonde beauty was happy reading instead of socializing. Her dramatic departure certainly wouldn't be earning her any new friends.

Jane clapped her hands twice as if summoning a pet. She looked around to see who was listening. "What we need to do now is get over to Mary's immediately. In a time of crisis, the best thing a friend can be is present. While she and I haven't always seen eye to eye, no one has ever accused me of not making myself available to those who need me. She'll see me coming—with my famous macaroni salad, of course—and probably break down in tears," she said proudly. A small group of women looked at each other and nodded their heads in admiration and approval.

While I agreed the sight of Jane Humphries and her accompanying minions might bring Mary to tears, it certainly wouldn't be with the sentiment Jane would be expecting. I had to curtail this mess before it became a full out disaster.

Jane was in the midst of organizing a troop of women, each being assigned to bring an accompanying dish, when I hastily interrupted. "Jane, your heart is in the right place but I must insist you stay away from Mary's, at least for the time being."

Jane looked offended. "Whatever for?"

"Do not take it the wrong way, Mary considers you

to be among her closest friends, I'm sure. But as I've seen her experience great loss before, I can tell you that she'll have barricaded herself away, unable to face anyone."

She glared at me. "Don't be silly. I insist we go over there and comfort her."

I stood my ground. "I really hate to argue against such a thoughtful, kind gesture, but please, let me at least head over first and make sure she is up to seeing anyone."

I could see that Jane wanted to have her way, but in the presence of so many ladies, she did not want to seem too pushy.

"I'd hardly consider myself *anyone*," she said grudgingly, "but if you think that would be better, then we won't go quite yet. I just want to do what's best for Mary."

I finally let out the breath I hadn't realized I was holding. "I will absolutely let Mary know you all are here for her and ready to help at a moment's notice."

I excused myself and started heading toward the exit before she changed her mind. I didn't think I could thwart her efforts to go see Mary for a second time.

There were a lot of small groupings of people, all discussing Charles at length. I tried to overhear as many conversations as I could as I made my way to the door. Most of them were similar. People were shocked and saddened, all wondering what happened. Even some of the staff seemed affected by the news.

When I left the building, there were three young women dressed in the club uniform smoking just outside the doors, talking in whispers. I guessed one of the requirements of working here must be to have a certain level of attraction, seeing as they were all quite pretty. I noticed they didn't seem as upset as anyone inside. I took two more steps before I paused and retraced my last few paces. A lightbulb had switched on in my head.

I approached the girls. When they noticed I was coming to talk to them, they all fumbled to put out their cigarettes and look proper. Each girl gave me her best winning smile.

One of them stepped forward. Her name ag read Sarah. "Is there something we can help you with, ma'am?" she asked pleasantly.

"Did you girls hear about Mr. Whitmore?" I asked, knowing the answer.

"Oh, yes, dreadful news, ma'am," Sarah replied, giving me a sympathetic smile.

I looked at each one individually. "Did any of you know Mr. Whitmore?"

The two girls not speaking exchanged a look. Sarah didn't flinch. "Of course, ma'am. He was a very well-known member. A charming man, people said. A shame he passed away before his time."

"Is that how you girls would describe him?" I asked.

A second, meaningful look was exchanged between the girls at the back, and this time Sarah blinked a few times and swallowed before answering. "I'm sorry, I'm not sure what you're asking."

I watched her carefully. "I'm just wondering if he was as well liked by the staff as he was by its members."

She faltered for a minute. "He was very friendly."

"Listen, I am not trying to put you on the spot here. There are a lot of tears being shed on his behalf inside the club." I leaned in closer and whispered, "But I didn't like the man. I was just wondering if I'm the only one. I saw you girls talking over here with dry eyes so I just thought I'd ask. I'm feeling a sudden burden of guilt for my dislike. Sorry for interrupting your conversation." I smiled apologetically at them and started to walk away.

"Wait," Sarah said. "You're not alone."

I turned back around to face them. One of the girls standing with Sarah kicked her foot purposefully. Sarah immediately closed her mouth. The kicker stepped forward.

"Sarah just means that we've seen all the members have good days and bad days. You probably caught him on a bad day just like a few of us have," she said. Her nametag read Melanie.

Sarah blushed. "That's it."

"Our break is over, we better be getting back inside," Melanie said now. "Nice talking with you, ma'am."

The girls smiled and hastily started toward the door.

"Hold on a minute, girls. I need one more minute of your time. It's important," I urged.

They all paused and looked at me nervously.

There was something they weren't telling me. I needed to convince these young women to talk. I decided to take a chance with honestly. "Charles Whitmore was married to one of my best friends. She is now being accused of killing him. I know that my friend did not do this. I need to find out who did so I can help prove it wasn't her. Everyone here seems to think he was a wonderful man. I need to know what they don't so I can figure out who did this and why. If there was a side of Charles that you girls knew that could give me some insight, it could help me and save my friend. Please." I hoped appealing to the bond of friendship sacred to so many young women would be enough.

The three of them looked at each other and nodded. It looked like my plea may have worked.

The first one I spoke to, Sarah, stepped up. "Okay, look, ma'am, Charles Whitmore was not a well-liked member by the staff, the female staff, at least."

"Why is that?" I asked, already suspecting the obvious.

"He said rude comments and, sometimes, if he had too much to drink, his hands would start to wander if one of us was nearby," she said.

"I'm sorry to hear that," I said sincerely.

The second young woman, Melanie, cleared her throat. "It's not really that uncommon to get a little tap on our bottom now and again. But Mr. Whitmore was different. He was always watching us and, if no one else were around, he'd try and corner us. He treated us like it was part of our job to smile even when his hands were groping us."

"What a terrible experience. Did it happen often?" I asked.

She looked down as if ashamed. "Yes, but like Sarah said before, it was worse when he was drinking. We'd usually try and make ourselves scarce then."

"Did any of you tell your boss?" I asked.

She scoffed. "Yes, a few times, and we were always told to avoid him when he was in that state. I don't think anyone really took the complaints seriously. He was pretty sneaky. He made sure no one else was around when he was at his worst."

"Besides," Sarah added, "It's just like you said. Everyone loved him. He was a very popular member."

Melanie tucked her hair behind her ear. "It would jeopardize our job to make a big deal about it."

"Is that what happened to Betty Smith?" I asked.

Sarah looked surprised by the question. "The former baker? Maybe."

"I was told she was caught in a compromising position with Charles, so she was let go," I said.

Sarah nodded. "That was a couple of summers ago when most of the waitresses, including myself, actually *liked* Mr. Whitmore. Well, at the beginning of the season anyways. You see, being a seasonal job, it takes a while to get to know the members, and we were all new that year except Betty."

"Did she like him?" I asked.

"I don't know. She kept to herself, mostly—she was older than the rest of us. But I remember she *did* warn us to stay away from him. We just thought she was jealous since he was nicer to the younger girls. When she got fired for being caught with him, we thought it confirmed our suspicion that she wanted him all to herself. But after she left he acted more aggressively and began to creep the rest of us out, too. That's when we realized she really had been trying to look out for us," Sarah said.

I shuddered. "What happened between them?"

"I don't know. None of us saw her again so we never got a chance to ask," she said.

Melanie tapped Sarah on the arm. "We've got to get back inside. Our break is over."

I clasped my hands together. "Thank you for trusting me."

Sarah gave me a little wave as she opened the door. "I hope it helps. Mrs. Whitmore is such a nice lady. I couldn't imagine her hurting anyone."

Melanie jeered. "Yeah, even Mr. Creepy."

The girls went inside and I headed toward the parking lot. I needed to find Betty Smith.

Chapter 15

Frank's car was parked in the driveway when I got home. I was glad because I felt like I hadn't seen Katherine and Robert in weeks, though it had really only been one—albeit long—day. I opened the door and Frank greeted me with a warm smile. My kids came over and gave me a big hug.

"Mom, are you okay?" Katherine asked.

I saw the worry in their faces and knew Frank must've told them what happened. "I'm fine, you guys. Don't worry. A terrible thing happened to Uncle Charles but the police are going to find out who did it, and that person will go to jail. I'm just going to be busy helping Aunt Mary through some tough times for a little while, okay?"

"Of course, Mom," Robert said.

"What you guys have been up to?" I asked.

"We went to see Peter Pan. It was amazing," Robert told me.

"Yeah, it was good, Mom." Katharine said. "At first, I thought the movie might be a bit juvenile but it was really exciting!"

"I'm glad you guys enjoyed it. I want to hear all about it at lunch. I'm going to make fried egg sandwiches with some canned ham. I hope you guys are hungry," I said.

"Always, Mom," Robert reminded me.

"Great, why don't you both go enjoy the sunshine and I'll call you when it's ready."

"Okay, Mom," Katharine said and she and Robert headed into the backyard.

When they were outside, I started preparing lunch. Frank had surprised me a few months ago, renovating the kitchen. It was so contemporary, complete with turquoise cupboards and speckled grey Formica counters. It sometimes cheered me up just being in the bright surroundings, but not today. Frank asked how I was really doing but I didn't want to worry him.

"Good," I said too cheerily, "I learned a lot today. I'm confident we're—I mean the police—are going to find the killer."

Frank's look of concern was back. My idea to stay positive backfired. It seemed to make him worry more.

"You learned a lot about what? Are you meddling, Izzy?"

"No, of course not," I said. *Not really, anyways.*

Lunch was made in no time and I sat down with Frank and the kids for a nice meal. Before I went out again, we all spent some time playing a few card games. I knew I was going to be busy over the next few days so I wanted to make sure I had time with my family so they didn't feel neglected. I could tell the kids were worried about me since there was not one single complaint about how long it took me to strategize my hand. It was a good tip to remember for future game nights.

Later in the afternoon, I called Mary's house and briefly spoke to Mrs. Collins. She said both Ava and Jo were taking a short rest as ordered by her. I told her I would be by the house shortly and headed out.

When I arrived at Mary's, it was quiet. Ava and Jo were still sleeping. I thought it was a good opportunity to talk to Mrs. Collins on my own. Mary and Charles had a very small household staff. In fact, Mrs. Collins was the only full-time employee. On occasion, she would request some additional help to do a top-to-bottom clean, or prepare for a large dinner party, but most of the time she fared well on her own. With no children and an empty house at lunchtime—Charles was presumably at the office and Mary normally had lunch plans—food preparation was restricted mainly to breakfast and dinner, giving her the rest of the time to take care of the large home.

I wanted to ask Mrs. Collins about Charles. As I approached her in the laundry room, I felt a little awkward. "Excuse me, Mrs. Collins, can I make you a cup of tea?" It occurred to me this was probably the first time I ever actually invited Mrs. Collins to sit down.

It must've struck her as odd, too. She looked quite surprised. "I never say no to a spot of tea, dear. But go on and sit. I'll make it," she said as she set the dial of the washer. "Would you like some biscuits with that?"

I smiled. "I never say no to biscuits."

She nodded. "Won't be long," she noted, dismissing me from the room.

I went into the kitchen and looked around for the kettle. Before I could find it, Mrs. Collins had it filling with water, insisting for a second time that I take a seat. A minute later, the tea was steeping and I was eating a cookie. Mrs. Collins then sat down.

"What's on your mind, dear?" she asked.

"I just wanted to know your thoughts on what's happened," I said.

"I am starting to feel like a broken record, repeating myself. First, the police ask me, then Ava and Jo, and now you. I don't mind as much with you lot, of course. It's a terrible business what's happened. Poor Mr. Whitmore gone too soon," she said.

"So you were fond of Charles?" I wondered.

"Of course I was. He paid me on time, never overworked me, and he always treated me with kindness and respect. What more could you ask for?" she responded.

"I've just heard talk of him not always treating women very well. I was just wondering if you ever experienced that yourself.".

She looked offended. "Never. Perhaps the women you've spoke to were a little on the sensitive side."

"In what way?" I asked.

"I've had one or two young girls come to help me on occasion. It's been mentioned to me that Mr. Whitmore was a little too friendly. I told the girls not to worry about how friendly he was and just get about their work," she continued. "If they paid near the attention to the floors as they did a sideways smile, they would see the reflection of their *own* face rather than worrying about someone else's."

"Is that all? An unwelcome look?" I questioned.

"I'm sure it wasn't much more or I would've heard about that too, dear," she dismissed.

"What about Charles and Mary's relationship?"

She didn't look pleased by the question. "What about it?"

"Would you say there was any cause for concern? Were they getting along all right recently?"

"I will tell you—as I told everyone else who's asked me—it is my job to oversee the *house* not its *residents*. As you are a close friend of Mrs. Whitmore's, I would assume you would know of any trouble already," she lectured me, giving nothing away.

I appealed to her. "I know Mary didn't kill him, Mrs.

Collins. I'm just trying to sort out the whole mess of it. I don't want to press Mary too much. She's stressed and overwhelmed right now. I need to make sure there's nothing more damaging regarding the Whitmore's relationship than what she's told me. I can't effectively help Mary if I don't know the whole truth."

She looked me in the eye and licked her lips. "Because the lady trusts you, I am indulging your questions and answering them with as much truth as I am comfortable. Let me put it this way: Mr. Whitmore's behavior was no better or worse toward the Mrs. than it had been since I've been employed with the family. If she was going to kill him for it, she would've done so years ago."

Her words were unsettling but her tone was so earnest, it struck me as almost comical. "Geez, I can pretty much guarantee that won't be the next Hallmark slogan." Mrs. Collins had never really cared for my humor. That moment was no exception.

Luckily she ignored my bad joke and persisted in answering. "There was one fact that I mentioned to the police that I will also share with you."

"What is it?" I asked.

"I overheard Charles talking to someone on the phone not long ago about a meeting," she told me.

"A meeting with who?" I asked.

"I don't know, but it had to do with work, I'm sure. I can always tell because his lawyer talk always sounded different from when he was speaking about anything else," she explained.

I didn't doubt her. "Do you know what it was in regards to?"

"Well, yes, that's why I brought it up. Charles was talking about how angry Mr. Stormwell would be when he found out about something or other. Can't tell you exactly what it was he was talking about, but I *can* tell you he seemed very pleased it would be upsetting to Mr. Stormwell," she recalled.

I clapped my hands together. "Mrs. Collins, you're brilliant. That could be extremely important."

"I suppose so, dear. I've said my piece now, and I won't say another word about Charles or his business, in or out of the house. Do you understand?" she asked pointedly.

"Yes, of course. Thank you."

"Now, I need to go press the drapes," she said, getting up, having finished her tea with surprising speed.

"W—wait—" I sputtered, when suddenly an idea flashed before me, "Mrs. Collins, I just have one more question and it has nothing to do with the state of the Whitmore's marriage, I promise." *Not directly anyways.*

"Yes, Isabelle, what is it?" she said, clearly growing bothered by my persisting questions.

"I know that you are more of a cook than a baker, so I wanted to know if you could recommend a bakery nearby?"

Her shoulders seemed to decompress when I changed topics and she smiled a little, "Now that's more like it, dear. Yes, of course I know a few. But I want to first clarify I can bake as well as cook but with no one here that really appreciates a nice dessert, I keep my baking to strictly breads and scones. For anything sweet, there are a few places I would go. What sort of thing do you fancy?"

I racked my brain quickly and answered confidently. "I was thinking of something rich and sweet, maybe a tart or a flan?"

"Lots of places around here make a nice pie, but a small bakery opened up on Kerr Street near Shoreline Road not long ago and, while the pastry chef put me off at first, once I tried her caramel custard flan, I was sold," she informed me.

"Why were you put off at first?" I asked.

"Well, the woman running the bakery is so young and attractive, I doubted she had the skill some of those dishes can require. I was wrong. She could go up against any flan creator I've ever come across."

"Thank you, Mrs. Collins," I said, standing up and giving her a hand a meaningful squeeze. "You've helped me more than you know."

"Okay, dear," she said, looking at me a little warily. "Go on then, I've got a full day ahead of me."

I briefly regretted showing Mrs. Collins how grateful I was because I thought it worried her, as if she gave something away she shouldn't have. But I couldn't hide the joy I was feeling, as I was quite certain I now knew where I could find the elusive Betty Smith.

I couldn't find the coffee pot so I settled for a second cup of tea. I wandered out to the backyard and before I took my first sip, I heard a sound overhead. I looked up and saw Ava waving at me from the bedroom window. She asked me to turn the kettle back on and said she'd be down in a jiff. I was anxious to tell Ava and Jo everything I had learned this morning. I walked back inside only to see her and Jo on the steps. I could tell they had things to tell me, too.

Ava and Jo grabbed a mug of tea and we headed back outside. It was another beautiful day, with the sun reflecting off the ocean, emphasizing the afternoon sun.

"Am I the only person being blinded here?" Ava asked, as she squinted at us for added emphasis.

"I seem to remember, just a few months ago, you complaining about the lack of sun, Ava," I replied.

She was walking with her hands outright, as if she no longer had use of her eyesight. "I suppose Mother Nature is having her revenge."

I grabbed her arm and led her to some nearby white, metal garden chairs arranged in a circle, under a tree. I helped her into one and then Jo and I sat down. "Speaking of revenge, I have a few things I want to tell you guys about."

Ava immediately regained her vision and pointed her notably long index finger at me. "Us first!" Then she dramatically whipped her arm to the side and aimed the lengthy digit at Jo. "Our city slicker here has taken a page out of your detective manual and come up with what we believe could be a solid clue."

Jo cleared her throat and looked calmly at me. "We don't know if it's really a *clue*," she clarified, "but it may be worth looking into."

"You've got my attention. What is it?" I asked.

"Bad news first: our talk with Mrs. Collins wasn't exactly illuminating. All she would really say is that she doesn't believe Mary is guilty and she has no idea who is," Jo said.

I raised my eyebrows. "I also tried to bend her policy of strict confidentiality with little success."

Ava nodded. "She's loyal and proud. That makes for a tough code to crack,"

Jo looked disappointed. "I thought she'd be more co-operative."

I felt confident I knew why Mrs. Collins was keeping things so close to the chest. "I think it's a response to the unexpected police interview she had. She might see it as protecting us, as well as Mary. The less we know, maybe, the better she thinks it is. That way we are not hiding anything if we get questioned, too."

"But that suggests there's something to hide," Jo countered.

Ava looked at me. "Jo's right. Do you think Mary is keeping something from us?"

I hesitated. "No, I mean, not anything like she killed Charles. But I think there is more that we could learn.

Obviously, Mrs. Collins isn't going to be the one to tell us so I'm going to go and ask Mary some more personal questions. I feel like we're not seeing the whole picture yet."

"What do you mean?" Ava asked.

I bit my lip. "I don't think we know everything we need to about Charles. And *that* could be preventing us from finding out what really happened."

Ava cocked her head to the side. "What exactly did you find out this morning, Izzy?"

I filled them in on what I had learned. They listened quietly. Ava had a look of concern and Jo's face showed clear disappointment.

"Jo," I asked. "When you lived here, did Charles ever act differently toward you, make you feel uncomfortable?"

"Not at all." Jo flushed. "I had come to think of Charles more like a father figure, or a generous uncle. I'm astounded by what people are saying. If it's true, he certainly never tried anything on me."

"Do you think that discredits what we've been told? Could it be that multiple women have misconstrued Charles's behavior?" I wondered out loud.

Jo's face looked hopeful. "It's possible. Maybe there's a more innocent explanation. Some sort of miscommunication?"

Ava scoffed. "Are you two pulling my leg?"

"What do you mean?" I asked.

She frowned at both of us. "This whole Charles innocence thing. Seriously, why do I always have to set you two straight?" she said, sounding annoyed.

I shrugged. "Still lost."

Her frown turned to a look of disbelief. "Have you two never heard of the hamburger rule?"

"Please enlighten us," I begged.

"Don't get your meat from the same place you store your bread?" Ava offered.

"Could you expand on that?" Jo asked.

Ava sighed. "Charles was not a stupid man. Do you really think he would try his twisted romantic charms on Jo, his wife's best friend, in their own home?"

I ran my hands through my hair. "Okay, I see what you're saying. You've got a point."

Ava looked relieved. "Charles would know Mary would never stand for that. There had to be a layer of separation."

She made a good argument. "You're right," I said, "He'd know where he could and couldn't get away with it."

"Exactly," Ava agreed. "It sounds like Charles may have had a few different sides to him, and I think we can assume we knew only the one he wanted us to see."

I folded my arms and smiled at her. "Your cynicism gives you an insightful edge, my friend."

She bounced in her seat. "That brings me back to what I started telling you before. Jo found something in the house that could lead us to finding out just how different some of those sides of Charles could be."

"I'm listening," I said.

"Jo, why don't you tell Izzy what you found," Ava offered.

"Okay, again, it could be nothing," Jo warned.

Ava leaned toward me. "Unlikely," she whispered.

"It's a pack of matches," Jo said as she pulled it out from her pocket and showed it to me.

"Okay..." I said, looking at it. "I don't get it. What is significant about that? A pack of plain black matches."

"Well, that's just it. To the uninitiated, that's all it is. But if you look closer you'll see a small upside down heart in the corner," she noted.

I saw it. "What does it mean?"

"There is only one place that gives out those particular matches. It's called the Casino Theatre. It's on Queen Street—on the far side of town," Jo informed me.

"Why does that sound remotely familiar?" I asked, racking my brain.

"If you read the papers, it comes up from time to time," Jo said.

Ava leaned toward me again. "In the naughty section." Ava licked her upper lip.

I was confused. "I'm lost again."

"It's a burlesque theater," Jo informed me. "The symbol is a heart right side up but a spade upside down. Only patrons of the risqué—some say—obscene theater would recognize it. I noticed the matches sitting on top of the fireplace in the den."

"And why is it that *you* recognize it?" I asked.

Jo blushed. "It's just one of the perks of working at a newspaper. You learn tidbits of information on some of the most unexpected of things. One of the writers is doing a piece on the theater and he was talking about it."

"Jo, you're a star. This could be just the break we need," I said enthusiastically. "The matches could only have belonged to Charles. We need to go there and poke around."

Jo looked doubtful. "Do you really think this could lead to something?"

"Absolutely," I replied confidently, "If there was ever a place for an assumed gentleman to feel unleashed— to lose his façade of 'gentle' and act…well, disrespectfully, that is it."

"When should we go?" Jo asked without hesitation.

"Tonight," I answered.

Jo rubbed her forehead. "I can't. I promised Mrs. Collins I'd help gather some of Mary's things for her so she could bring them to her in the morning."

"Don't worry, Jo," Ava piped in. "Izzy and I will go. You stay here. I'm sure two of us going there will be awkward enough. Three of us would seem downright bizarre. We want to raise as little attention to ourselves as possible."

"Ava's right. It's good to have someone at the house anyways in case Mary needs us," I said.

"All right, I guess," Jo said, unconvinced.

Ava looked at Jo with a hint of a smile. "You look almost disappointed."

Jo blushed again. This time it was a deep crimson. "Okay, I'll admit, I'm a little curious."

Ava leaned over and jabbed her with an elbow. "We'll let you know if it's worth a follow up visit."

I decided right about then I was going to call Frank and let him know I'd be spending the night at Mary's.

Chapter 16

It didn't take Ava and me long to get across town. Traffic was never all that busy. It would've been a pleasant drive under better circumstances. I looked at the sun setting over the ocean and thought about how beautiful it looked.

"So, what kind of scene do you expect to find? It's a little out of my usual Sunday night pattern," Ava joked.

"I really don't know what to expect. All I have to reference is the movies. I think we can agree it may not meet Hollywood standards."

"In my imagination, everyone is going to be in black and white and have mobster suits with New York accents. Do you think we're going to see real-life gangsters?"

"I'm *guessing* that Twin Oaks criminals may not be

as flashy as Al Capone was, but why are you asking me? I keep picturing men breaking out in chorus songs wearing matching sailor suits!"

Ava giggled. "Well, I'm looking forward to seeing what a real-life girlie theater looks like. It'll give us an inside view into a whole different world."

"That's true. People can have a lot of opinions about a place they've never been."

"What's the name of it again?" Ava asked.

"It's called the Casino Theatre," I answered. "It's on the corner of Queen and Bridge Street. We're almost there."

As we turned onto the street, we could see the Casino Theatre sign with a few questionable playbills displayed and men entering discreetly. It was a little intimidating but we came here for answers, and I was determined to get them. Ava looked around nervously as she got out of the car.

We walked up to the ticket booth where a grubby, older man was sitting behind a glass window. "Can I help you?" he asked cautiously.

"Um, yes, we would like two tickets to the burlesque show for tonight," I said confidently.

He looked us over skeptically. "Listen, ladies, we don't want any trouble here so if you're looking for your husbands, you'll just have to wait at home."

"We're not looking for anything, we just want to see a show," I said, trying to avoid meeting his filmy, textured eyes.

"Have you been here before?" he demanded, obviously suspicious of my attempt at nonchalance.

"Listen, bub," Ava demanded, "We may not look it, but we used to be dancers ourselves. We want to see what the next generation is doing."

I frowned at her and she stepped on my toe as she continued to flash a rather odd smile—I thought it was her attempt at demure—at the man in the ticket window. Whether or not he believed Ava's story I couldn't say, but either way he just shook his head and sold us the tickets.

"Really?" I said as we walked toward the entrance.

"Let's just get inside and see what we came to see," she replied.

We handed the uninterested doorman our tickets and in we went. The theater looked a little run down. It was bigger than I pictured, but I couldn't describe much of its decor because it was so dark. There was a large area of seating, just like at a regular movie theater, with a balcony on top. The seats were mostly taken up with men drinking beer and smoking cigarettes. The stage had an orchestra pit up at the front and the band could be heard warming up for the show.

We sat at the end of a row of seats, out of the way. At first, I was worried the clientele would notice us, and we'd be a bit of a spectacle. However, what I realized looking around was that nobody was here to make friends. Men kept to themselves. Nobody wanted to be recognized or have friendly conversations. They were strictly here to be entertained.

"It feels a bit seedy, doesn't it?" Ava remarked.

"It certainly doesn't have the sparkle and glitz I pictured from the movies," I agreed.

It was five minutes until show time when an announcer came out to welcome the patrons and introduce the act. The music started up shortly after and the dancers slowly came down the steps from the second floor, amid some cheers, jeers, and whistles. Attractive women dressed in corsets, feathers, and heavy make-up filled the stage. For the next hour, Ava and I sat quite mesmerized by the show. I could certainly see the appeal of it and found myself, at times, blushing in the dark. The somewhat rundown theater was transformed into a lively display of dance and entertainment.

When the show ended and the applause died off, men filtered out the doors into the dark night. Ava and I lingered, waiting for the last few men to leave.

"Okay, ladies, show's over, time to go home," said the same man said who sold us the tickets.

I could see no other choice but to follow his request, so we too went out into the night.

"That was really neat," Ava gushed, lit up with excitement.

"I'm surprised to say I agree with you. Those women are talented. It's a real skill." I was looking up and down the street. I spotted a small alley entrance attached to the theater. "C'mon," I said to Ava, "Let's go."

Ava didn't hesitate. She followed me down the narrow lane. I paused before knocking. "Can you let me ask the questions, please?"

"I just came for the entertainment, ask away," she agreed.

A door opened and a man slipped out of the theater. He had his head down and he brushed past us. I had just enough time to grab the door before it locked. Ava and I stepped inside.

There was such a bustle of activity, no one noticed us at first. There were a lot of people bustling around in just about every direction. Musicians were packing up their instruments and stagehands were taking down the set. The dancers seemed to be in less of a rush, however, many of them still in their costumes. I grabbed Ava's hand and we followed one of them. The dancer led us to an open area where several women were sitting in front of vanities, removing their makeup. There were three or four men lurking around, whom I assumed were spectators of the show. A few of the dancers began engaging them in conversation and the resulting flirtatious giggles made me feel uncomfortable. I wasn't sure what they were discussing was entirely legal. My guess was that the men were looking for a paid date.

One of the women looked up from her mirror and—finally—took notice of us, "Can I help you?" she asked suspiciously.

I hesitated. "I'm not sure. I have a few questions and I'm hoping you can help."

"We don't teach women your age how to dance, sorry, honey," she said dismissively.

"Oh, no, I couldn't imagine any amount of teaching could make this body do what you did out there," I said.

"Then what do you want?"

"I'm trying to help out a friend. You see it's her husband—" I started.

"Oh, geez, if your friend's husband didn't come home last night, call the police. We don't get involved in domestics," she sneered.

"He's not missing, he's dead!" Ava blurted out.

That got the attention of the room, and it suddenly went silent. All eyes were on us. Ava looked at me apologetically.

I stammered for a second and the woman who first addressed us smiled with thinly veiled disdain. "Okay, ladies, you have an audience. Spill the beans."

"My friend is telling the truth," I said. "A man is dead and nobody knows what happened to him. We're here because our friend is in trouble and we want to help. We have no idea what we're looking for. We found a pack of matches from your club and thought there was a chance it might lead to some answers. It's a long shot but we're asking for just a minute of your time."

She licked the inside corners of her mouth with the tip of her tongue. "We look out for each other around here. I respect that you are doing the same for your friend. We get hundreds of men in and out of here every day. I don't ask names or remember faces. But show me a picture anyways and I'll take a look," she said. "The name's Mag, by the way. C'mon girls, let's gather 'round and see if we know this guy."

A group of five or six women walked over to Mag's chair as I grabbed a photo from my purse of Charles I had taken from Mary's earlier. I passed it to her and they all stole a peek. Before Mag could say anything, one of the women elbowed the woman next to her and they exchanged a look of astonishment.

Mag clapped her hands, let her head fall back, and let out a loud cackle. "Well, well, looks like good ol' 'Cheering Charlie' finally got what was coming to him, eh, girls?"

A few of the girls nodded in agreement. They all seemed to have a look of cruel satisfaction.

I was taken aback. "You mean you recognize Charles?"

Mag looked at us. "Oh yes, we know him. Some of us better than others, but he's on all of our radars. So what happened? Did someone fight back with a killer right hook?" she said, not even trying to hold back the contempt in her voice.

I looked back at her earnestly. "I'm sorry, I don't follow."

"'Charlie liked to bring flowers and chocolates before the shows. He paid attention and applauded at the right time, praising our hard work. Then he liked to take a girl out to an expensive dinner, dropping a pretty penny on wine and food. Afterward, he'd bring her back to his car and try to have his way," she said, "He didn't like to be told no."

"That sounds a little sleazy," I admitted.

"What a dog," Ava added, trying to appeal to the girls.

"Yeah, well a lot of the men that come in here are different than they are at home. A little louder, a little ruder, they come here to blow off steam and break away from their day-to-day life. Once in a while you get a creep. But Charlie really had us fooled. We thought he was one of the good guys. What a laugh," she said.

"Had he come in recently?" I asked.

"As recent as last week, I think. Now, I've answered your questions. I don't want to talk about that louse anymore. It puts me in a bad mood. Time for you to split," she instructed and looked around. "Everyone get back to your own stations. The show's done for the night." She paused and looked at us in the reflection of her mirror, clearly not trying to hide the malice in her voice. "Go home," she growled.

"Can we ask you just a few more questions?" I begged.

"No." She got up from her chair and walked toward what could have been a shower room, never looking back.

I scoured the room. No one was paying us any more

attention. Ava and I stood there for another minute, feeling, once again, out of place and unwelcome. I approached another grouping of women. One of them looked at me. "You heard what Mag said. It's time for you to leave. No one else here is going to talk to you. Get lost."

Out of options, Ava and I walked toward the door. A petite brunette brushed against me and discreetly handed me a note, barely glancing at me as she passed. I waited until we were outside to read it.

Meet me in at the Crown Café in fifteen minutes. There's more you need to know. Don't be late.

I showed it to Ava. She let out a big sigh. "I know we came here for answers but I'm feeling more confused than ever."

"So am I. Let's get to the Crown Café and hope we get some of our questions answered," I said.

"Where the hell is that?" Ava asked.

"One more question I don't know the answer to. C'mon, let's find out," I said.

Chapter 17

We went into a milk shop and got directions. The Crown Cafe was just a few blocks away. The young woman who slipped me the note was already there, looking around nervously. I guessed she was in her early twenties but had lived a hard life. Her skin still had a light dusting of glitter on it from the show but under the harsh diner lights, her sallow complexion could clearly be seen underneath. Her blonde hair was thin, too, like her brittle frame, both suggesting a lack of basic care not usually seen in our affluent town. It made me sad, looking at what could've been a pretty young woman in another life. When she saw us, she did one last look around and sank down into a booth at the back of the restaurant so she couldn't be seen.

We walked back to where she was and sat down, both facing her.

She looked at Ava and then at me. "What I'm going to tell you could cost me my job. I can't afford that."

I felt grateful she was willing to take such a risk. "Whatever you tell us will remain strictly anonymous."

"I got your word?" she said, looking at me in eye, "'cause I'm all for doing the right thing but not if it lands me on the street. I need to take care of myself first. I don't have anyone else looking out for me."

"You have our word," I said, as Ava nodded in agreement.

"Okay, I'm going to trust you because the truth about that bastard should be known. I don't want him to be mourned or missed. Not by anyone. He don't deserve it," she said.

"What exactly is it that you know, Miss..." I prompted.

"My name don't matter. Just call me Bev," she said.

Butterflies were fluttering around in my stomach. "All right, if that makes you more comfortable, Bev."

Ava looked at me and then looked her. "You're scaring us a bit, Bev. Please, just tell us what you want us to know."

"It's not just what I know, it's what I experienced," she began, "I was one of the many girls Charlie has taken out. What Mag told you is true. He liked to wine and dine us girls, show us what a big man he is by flashing his money around, you know the type. But that kind of chivalry isn't usually given to us, so it's flattering. Afterward, it's like Mag said: he takes a girl back to his car and tries to have his way. But what she didn't tell you is *how* he tried to have his way. It wasn't like some excited high school boy who gets a little fresh. Charlie hits. He hits hard. His signature move is a punch to the head repeatedly and viciously. No bruises, just pain. Most girls give in, there and then. If they don't, he—literally—kicks them out of the car and acts as if they were a tease or something, never to acknowledge them again. If they give in, he invites them out again with his fake charm and the whole night repeats itself."

Ava and I looked at each other. This was much more disturbing than I expected. I didn't doubt that Charles was likely a creep, but was he really capable of being some sort of predator like she was describing?

"Which of the scenarios played out with you?" I asked.

"I got kicked out of his car and never looked at again. I was one of the lucky ones," Bev said sarcastically.

"That's quite a disturbing description of a man we've known for several years," I said.

Ava was frowning. "I won't pretend I liked the man but if Charles was such a terrible beast, why would any of the women working at the club accept an invitation from him?"

"There's certain rules that we are expected to follow in order to keep our jobs. Officially, we are not allowed to date the patrons. The managers don't want to deal with personal dramas that could come with a dancer/client relationship. They'll turn a blind eye if it's discreet. But if there's any trouble, the club will get rid of the dancer, and back the customer. The circumstance don't matter. Nice, huh?"

"But wouldn't there be enough women to warn one another about his behavior?" I asked.

"The slightest hint at badmouthing a big spender like Charlie would have any of us out on our ass in a New York Minute. So, sure, there's a few whispers and rumors, but in a business that sees women come and go, no job guaranteed beyond that night's whistles, not much is shared, at least not with the new girls."

I was trying to process what this woman was sharing with us. It was hard to discern if we should trust her or not. Could bitterness have clouded the truth?

"Why are you taking the risk of confiding all of this to us?" I asked.

"I may not have been able to do anything when he was alive, but when I heard you talking today, I felt like it was a chance to get the truth out," Bev stated harshly. "Charlie preyed on women who were lonely and desperate. He was manipulative, violent, and cruel. I want people to know it. I want *everyone* to know it. I said it before, Charlie doesn't deserve to be missed."

"Any chance you may be exaggerating a bit?" Ava asked cautiously, "That maybe he was more interested in someone else or decided he didn't like you? Rejection can make anyone feel angry."

Bev eyed us hatefully and then laughed. There was no joy in the sound. We just watched her awkwardly. She looked at us both and squinted her eyes. "I don't know who the bigger fool is, you for thinking Charlie may not deserve the fate he was given, or for me for telling you why he did and thinking you'd listen."

With that, she stood up and walked away. Neither one of us tried to stop her.

"That's a really angry person," Ava said quietly.

"Yes, it is. What do you think about her story?" I asked.

"It seems a little extreme to me. She made Charles sound like a monster." Ava shuddered. "I just can't picture it."

"Neither can I. Why would he hit a woman if she had already given a signal she was interested and game for a little fooling around?" I wondered.

"Unless the game to him was hitting her *and* fooling around," Ava suggested.

"True," I conceded.

We finished our coffee and headed home. I was relieved to be heading back to the nice side of town. As much as I liked trying new experiences, a few hours out tonight had been more than enough for me.

Chapter 18

The next day, Frank wanted to get up early and head to the shop. I made sure I was home by seven to help the kids get ready for day camp. Without mentioning the evening's events, I made breakfast for everyone and took the kids to the bus stop. It kind of felt as if I had a secret I was keeping from Frank. There hadn't been much time to tell him about where I'd been the night before, but I hadn't exactly looked for the opportunity to do so, either. I figured there was plenty of time to fill him in later.

Once he and the kids were off, I had the day to myself. There was a lot I wanted to do. I immediately called Charles's law office and spoke to Erica. It had only been a few days since we met but I was glad to hear her voice.

She was another close friend of Mary's and could be a big help with our investigation. She spoke quietly on the phone. I asked her if I could come by. She said yes but warned me the office was in disorder.

I got into my car and headed to the law office. I wasn't sure if I'd have the chance to speak to Charles's business partner, William Stormwell, but just talking to Erica could provide me with a lot of insight into what was happening there. No one knew what was going on more than the person who was in the center of it all. Erica saw all the documents, typed all the letters, and answered all the calls. That was in addition, of course, to keeping track of schedules and being a constant presence at the office.

When I arrived, I knew why Erica had been quiet on the phone. The police were here, going through Charles's desk and looking through his papers. I ran into Detective Jones.

"Mrs. Walsh, I thought we had a deal," he said.

I felt a little sheepish. "I'm sorry, Detective, I'm not sure what you mean."

His eyebrows lifted, and wrinkles of doubt spread across his forehead. "You are supposed to be keeping your nose out of my investigation."

"I'm just here to visit Erica. She's a friend of mine and I wanted to see how she's holding up."

He didn't say anything. He just continued to look at me, trying to gauge whether I was telling the truth. It was a little unnerving.

"I've always been one who prefers face to face communication, especially in such delicate situations," I blurted out awkwardly.

He rolled his eyes. "Just stay out of our way, please, Mrs. Walsh."

"I promise," I said with more sincerity.

"I've heard that before. Don't think, because you eluded my notice at the golf club the other day, that I didn't see your little red convertible, by the way."

I must've looked as surprised as I felt because he added, "Yeah, I'm smarter than I look. Comes in handy in my business. If you're going to try your hand at amateur detective, you may want to consider a more discreet vehicle."

I felt quite confident my face now matched the color of the indiscreet little red convertible. "I apologize Detective Jones, I mean no disrespect. I'm just trying to help my friend."

"I know you are, Mrs. Walsh. But this is a grave situation and not one to be made light of," he said.

"Of course, Detective. I understand the severity."

He looked at me intently, again. I didn't know if all detectives had his touch, but I felt like he could decode even my deepest thoughts without a word. He ended our conversation with a nod and went back to work. I watched what the detective was doing in the hopes of getting some direction. He was sifting through documents but didn't seem to be paying much attention to them. Instead, he was focused on a closed door within the office.

He kept looking up at it as if waiting for something. When the door opened a minute later and Erica emerged, he jumped at the opportunity to walk in. He sat down on a chair on the opposite side of a desk from where an older, well-dressed man sat looking stressed and tired. I knew immediately that it could only be William Stormwell.

Erica was back at her desk, talking on the phone. She hadn't noticed me yet. I decided to press my luck and slipped into the room with Detective Jones. As I walked in, Mr. Stormwell looked up at me. That prompted the detective to turn around. When he saw me, I could almost discern the shadow of a smile.

"Mr. Stormwell, let me introduce you to my new friend here, in case you haven't met. This is the very persistent Mrs. Walsh. She is a close friend of Mrs. Whitmore's and is just here to visit your secretary as you can see," he said with thick sarcasm.

I ignored his tone. "Hello."

Mr. Stormwell asked me about Mary. "How is she doing? I've been thinking about her, wondering how she's holding up through this terrible ordeal."

I was surprised by his sincerity. "Mary is a strong woman," I said, "She is faring well under the circumstances."

"Mr. Stormwell, let's get back to why *I'm* here if that's okay with you and Mrs. Walsh," Detective Jones said as he shot me a look of warning.

"Sorry, Officer, I want to cooperate and help in any way I can," Mr. Stormwell replied.

"Sure, and it's Detective Jones by the way."

"Of course, sorry, Detective," Mr. Stormwell said politely.

Detective Jones nodded in acknowledgement of the apology. "Now, can you describe your relationship with Mr. Whitmore?"

"Yes, we've known each other for several years, since college, in fact. Over that time, we worked together at a large firm in New York before deciding to become partners and open up our own firm here in Twin Oaks. While Charles and I were quite different personally, we got along well and respected one another's work tremendously. He was a sharp and talented lawyer." He spoke in an eloquent manner, with clear pronunciation and an authoritative tone.

"Was there any case he had been working on recently that was ruffling feathers or causing anyone to be upset with him?" the detective asked.

"No. I understand in your line of work, you must deal with a lot of angry, troubled, people. But we are corporate not criminal lawyers. As such, we work on business deals, specializing in European and American mergers. There were certainly times we would have frustrated parties, but none that I could see leading to the barbaric end of my partner, sir."

Detective Jones stopped asking questions for a moment and just sat. It must be a tactic. "Okay, let me ask you this then. The relationship you describe between yourself and your former partner sounds seamless. So why would Mr. Whitmore be considering severing your partnership?"

The well-spoken lawyer looked indignant. "That is preposterous. He was doing no such thing. We have talked in the past of possibly hiring on a few more associates to *expand* our firm. There has never been any talk of a *cessation* of our firm. We run a very successful business."

The detective's eyes were wide open. "Can I assume you wouldn't have been too happy if Mr. Whitmore decided to move on to greener pastures?"

Now it was Mr. Stormwell's face that turned red. "He wouldn't do that. It would be foolish. As I just said, we are a very successful business and had a great partnership."

"It seems to me that you may have been a little old fashioned and dull for the likes of Mr. Whitmore," Detective Jones commented.

I could see he was going out of his way to aggravate Mr. Stormwell. Smart move. It was working.

Mr. Stormwell stood up aggressively. "Just because you are used to a less refined manner than mine, don't be fooled. Mr. Whitmore was certainly flashier, but I can be a shark when I need to be. Do not underestimate me, Detective Jones." His eyes flashed and his voice shook. His behavior was a striking departure from the gentle manner in which he first spoke.

"Point taken. That's all I wanted to know." Detective Jones looked smug as he stood up, "Don't cross the pond, or even the state, Mr. Stormwell. I may have more questions for you in the days to come."

Mr. Stormwell appeared angry and flustered. He had let the detective get under his skin and it looked like he had already come to regret it. I thought about asking a few questions of my own but held off. I smiled sympathetically at Mr. Stormwell from the doorway. He meekly returned the expression. I walked out of his office, past Detective Jones who was now talking to another officer, and toward a familiar face. Erica was sitting at her desk typing, seemingly oblivious to the police officers and growing chaos in the office.

As I approached her, she looked up and smiled. "Finally, a friendly face," she said, "It's good to see you, Isabelle."

"Erica, in a sea of chaos, you look like a picture of calm."

"It's a little crazy around here. But I learned that when there's work that needs to be done, it's important to focus. It certainly isn't the first time I've needed to tune out distraction."

Her professionalism and dedication impressed me. "I see you're busy, but I was hoping to get just a few minutes of your time. I have some questions and you're the only person who can answer them."

"You've got impeccable timing. I was just thinking I could really use a break and some coffee. There's a little shop just up the block. Care to join me?" she asked.

"Sounds like a brilliant idea. I'd love to," I said gratefully.

Erica grabbed her smart blue tailored jacket and we left. It was nice to get away from the overcrowded office.

Chapter 19

The cafe was small but there was ample seating. She followed me in and I chose a booth by the window out of habit. I like to people watch. It's one of my favorite pastimes. But today there was no time for such reverie. I focused on Erica.

A waitress came by and we each ordered a coffee and a bagel. I was glad to have Erica's undivided attention. She could hold an important piece of this puzzle. First, though, she wanted to know how Mary was doing. I told her what I'd been telling everyone who inquired: she was a strong woman doing the best she could under the circumstances. That seemed to comfort Erica a little. I knew she didn't have much time so I pressed on.

"I know as the secretary and office manager you are

the reason things run smoothly at the office," I began.

Erica smiled. "Yes, I'm a busy woman, you could say. It gives me a headache just looking at the mess the police have managed to make in just one day. Not that I'm complaining. They need to do their job. If there is anything that will help free Mary of the false charges against her, I encourage them to find it."

"Do you think they'll find anything?" I asked.

"I'm not sure, to be perfectly honest. There were, of course, people who did not like Charles. He was a great negotiator so our clients sometimes got more than their fair share in settlement and contract deals, I imagine. There's a lot of money involved in some of the business transactions our firm oversees, but nothing stands out as a particular motive to want Charles dead. That would seem extreme and very unlikely. I mean, at the end of the day, it is just business."

"What about the ending of a partnership?" I asked.

She looked uncharacteristically expressive in the surprise she displayed. "Are you talking about Charles and William?"

"Yes," I said simply.

"I haven't heard anything about it. There didn't seem to be any imminent changes happening in the office."

"How was their relationship?" I asked, not letting it go.

"It seemed fine. They worked well together. William was happy. I assume Charles was, as well."

"Why weren't you as close to Charles?" I wondered.

"When I was still in New York and looking for a quieter place to settle down, William hired me for their firm. I had worked with him on various legal proceedings before. He really went out of his way to help me. We simply remained close," she explained.

"How would William react if Charles were to leave the firm?" I asked.

"He'd be upset, of course. Plus, it wouldn't look good to the clients. People don't like to see a lot of changes in their law firm. They like it to run smoothly. Any major restructuring could put the firm's business in jeopardy. Especially since half of clients were represented specifically by Charles," she admitted.

"Was it hard for them to establish the firm?" I asked.

"International business law is a specialized and complicated area. Starting a small, independent firm with that type of clientele is tough. But William and Charles met at law school and they shared a dream. Together they worked hard and became exceptional lawyers. So, yes, there were a lot of long hours at the beginning but the firm has been successful for years now," she explained.

"The way you describe it, I would think they would be very close. But they don't seem to be. Am I wrong?"

"Listen, Isabelle, I don't think it's my place to really get into the nature of their relationship any more than I already have. I would just leave it alone if I were you," she said earnestly.

"Did something happen to sour that initial affinity?" I pushed.

Erica shifted in her seat and looked dismayed. "This is really none of your business, Isabelle. If I thought in any way that William could be responsible for Charles's death, I would be the first to speak up and say so. Don't forget that Mary is my friend, too. But you're looking down the wrong path."

"Am I? I'm not so sure. That's something I need to determine on my own. If you're not comfortable telling me, I could ask Mr. Stormwell."

Erica sighed. "No, he's under so much pressure already. I don't want him to have any more stress on top of that. If you are determined to be persistent, as I see you are, I will tell you. As I mentioned, Charles and William were good friends at law school. They remained close after graduating and spent their first few years at the same law firm as junior lawyers in New York. As they gained experience and knowledge, they decided to open a firm in Twin Oaks. When the war broke out, their business was still young and was under financial strain as many young businesses are. At the same time, Charles's much younger brother, Cary, decided to enlist in the navy. He pressured Charles to do the same. Cary felt that, since both he and Charles were accomplished at sailing and being on the water, they could be a real help to the cause, especially since so many of the young soldiers enlisting didn't have as much experience. Charles was torn between supporting his brother and following his personal dream and career pursuits."

"Tough choice," I commented. "That must've been a very hard decision."

"I'm sure it was. There was also pressure from William. He and Charles had both taken a big risk leaving good jobs at a reputable firm to open a small practice on their own. If Charles had signed on to go overseas and fight in the war, it would've ruined any chance of success. You see, both he and William were working day and night for those first few years just to make ends meet. William wouldn't have been able to maintain the efforts required to make it work on his own. From what I understand, he told Charles directly that his loyalty *must* remain with the new firm and, in the end, Charles agreed. He made the decision to stay home and focus on his career."

"How did his brother react to his decision?"

"Cary called Charles a coward, and they had a falling out before he left to join the fight. Tragically, as with so many brave soldiers in the war, he lost his life in battle. Charles seemed to blame himself for not being there, as if he could've prevented his brother's death. He never forgave himself. He *also* never forgave William. Their relationship disintegrated into one of mere business. William tried to mend their friendship but Charles was too heartbroken and angry over his brother's death to allow it. Eventually, William let it go and accepted that Charles would now be his business partner and nothing more," Erica concluded.

"That's really unfortunate. William could've been such a source of comfort and consolation to Charles if he'd have let him," I said.

"You're right. Instead, Charles seemed to build a shell around himself and his caring, generous spirit, once so prevalent, seemed lost," Erica said.

"That's when I first met Mary, during the war," I told Erica, "She used to talk about Charles so differently then. They had been married for quite a while and she seemed to love him dearly. She was fairly private about her personal life, but I *do* remember that."

"I would guess it would've changed him at home just as much, if not more, than at the office. But that's something you'd have to ask Mary about, of course."

"Yes, of course," I said, finding myself a little lost in thought.

"Please tell me your questions have been answered and I am free to return to work, Isabelle," Erica pleaded. "I don't want William to start wondering where I've gone. He really needs me right now."

"Of course, Erica. Thank you so much for telling me more about the history between William and Charles. It helps me understand things a little better."

"You're welcome. If you want to find out any more about Charles, you may want to go back to the golf club. That's where you can find his closest friends. They will likely be there in about an hour for their Monday afternoon game."

It was a good suggestion. "How would I go about finding them?"

"Go to the club lounge where they serve drinks. That's where the men spend the majority of their time," she informed me.

"There are lots of women who play golf these days too, aren't there?" I asked.

"Yes, but it's mostly segregated between the sexes. Before heading out on the course, they usually met at the unofficial men-only lounge for a little socializing," she said.

"Women are not welcome to join them?"

"Have you never heard the acronym GOLF?" she asked me.

I shook my head to indicate no.

"*Gentlemen Only Ladies Forbidden,*" she explained. "It outlines a popular sentiment and a rule that Charles and his friends stuck to."

I was quite surprised. "That sounds awfully juvenile."

"Yes, it seemed that way to me, as well. I often had to go there to get Charles to sign documents or look over papers, and any time I walked into the lounge to find him, he and his friends would be quite put off. Their conversation would cease and they would eye me with suspicion. It was all I could do not to roll my eyes. Of course, they were cordial and polite but I was never asked to stay for tea. So, I don't know how much they'll talk to you, but they're your best bet if you're trying to find his confidantes."

"Interesting," I noted. "I'll keep that in mind."

We walked back to the office quietly.

"Before I go, I just have one more question," I said.

"What is it?" Erica asked, growing visibly worn down by the questions I had for her.

"Is there anything else you could tell me that struck you as unusual or odd over the last few months that could shed some light on what has happened?" I asked.

Erica stopped walking suddenly and looked at me, her eyes shining with renewed energy. "I hadn't really thought about it but now that you ask, there is one thing."

"What is it?" I asked anxiously.

She leaned in closely and spoke quietly as if to make sure no one could overhear. "A man called a few days before Charles was killed. He was angry and rude, demanding to know where Charles was and wanting to know his phone number and address."

"What did you do?"

"I said I wasn't at liberty to give out that sort of information and asked if there was anything *I* could do to help. But he laughed in a loud and bitter way and said the only one who would need help is Mr. Whitmore when he was through with him," she said, "My goodness, I can't believe I had forgotten about that call. I guess I should tell the police."

"Sounds like a good lead. Any idea who it might have been?" I asked.

She shook her head. "No, *but* if it were a client I would've recognized the voice. I think it was something more personal."

Poor Charles may have crossed the wrong man, after all. We ran into Detective Jones as he was leaving the office. Erica explained she had something she'd forgotten to tell him. They went back inside together. I decided to wait around outside. When Detective Jones emerged a few minutes later, I approached him.

He greeted me with a smile. I checked behind me to see if it was meant for someone else. "Mrs. Walsh, I may regret saying this, but you have helped uncover a possible new lead, so—nice work. I'm not convinced Mary Whitmore is innocent but I'm a thorough investigator and I'm fair. So, if you manage to find any more leads, let me know. You may prove to be more of a help than a hindrance, after all. Crazier things have been known to happen, I suppose."

I returned his smile proudly. "I take that as a great compliment, Detective."

"Don't let it get to your head. I still want you to stay out of my way *and* out of danger. Okay?"

"I will," I promised.

He tipped his hat. "You've just made my day a lot busier so I better be off. I'm sure I'll be seeing you." With that he strolled away to his nearby car.

Chapter 20

I went straight over to Mary's where I found Ava and Jo finishing breakfast. They were showered and eager to start the day. I told them about Erica's disturbing call.

Jo looked down at her watch. "Geez, Izzy, you've been busy," she said. "Especially considering the hour you got back last night."

Ava didn't look nearly as surprised. "Once you have an idea in your head, there's certainly no stopping you."

We left the kitchen and walked toward the front entrance. Jo crossed her arms. "There sure doesn't seem to be any shortage of motives for hurting Charles. I was worried we may not be able to find any viable suspects, but so far, our problem seems just the opposite."

Ava stopped to reapply her lipstick in a hallway mirror. She looked at us in the reflection. "We may even have a hard time narrowing it down to just one!"

I bit my lip. "There were a lot of people who didn't like him."

"There are a lot of people I don't like, either," Jo reminded us. "But there's a big stretch between dislike and murder."

Ava cleared her throat. "But the *way* Charles crossed some of these people probably created feelings going way beyond dislike."

Jo sighed. "Ava's right, Izzy. Charles was always kind to me but it sure sounds like he had his share of enemies."

I couldn't argue. "I'd like to get more insight into his life at the golf club."

Jo perked up. "I was pretty friendly with some of the members when I lived with Mary and Charles. I could go there today and find out if there are any new theories floating around. It might lead to something."

I nodded. "That would be great, Jo."

Ava leaned toward me. "And what is on the agenda for us today, boss?"

I grinned. "I thought you and I might get some fresh baked flan."

"I know just the place," Ava said with a wink. "There's a bakery I heard about down on Kerr Street."

I felt certain the day would bring more clarity. "Sounds perfect."

We dropped Jo off at the club and agreed to pick her up after lunch. Ava and I headed to Kerr Street. It was not hard to find. Even before going in, the unmistakable wafting of fresh baked bread filled my nose. It was enough to make my stomach perk up and rumble. No one ever accused me of having a small appetite.

Ava grinned at me "Maybe we should buy some baked goods before asking questions," Ava said, grinning, "I would hate to miss out on baking that smells so good!"

A cute blonde woman with blue eyes and rosy cheeks was busy working behind the counter when we walked in. She had short bangs that framed her round face. The rest of her hair was long and pulled neatly back in a ponytail. She was pulling out some appetizing French loaves from an oven and placing them on a cooling rack.

She gave us a welcoming smile. "Good morning, ladies."

"Good morning," Ava and I said in unison.

"What can I get for you this morning?" she asked.

It looked like Ava had forgotten why we were here. "There are so many tempting things, it's hard to decide."

The attractive baker looked pleased. "Everything is fresh. I baked some San Francisco sourdough this morning that will knock your socks off. These baguettes may need a little time to cool but if you can wait a few minutes, they'll be ready to wrap up, as well. And, of course, my signature desserts," she informed us, pointing out a colorful display of pastries.

Ava examined everything with hungry eyes. "What time do you have to get up to prepare all of this?"

"I beat the sun every morning. A fresh cup of coffee with a quick read of the paper and I'm ready to go," she told us.

I always loved the idea of getting up that early—that is, until I tried it. I was like a grumpy zombie. Frank asked me not to attempt it again. "That is impressive," I said.

"I love what I do and I never take it for granted. When you live your dream, there's no need to waste the day lazing about," she told us, as she prepared to work on some other culinary task.

"How inspiring," Ava said. "Do you and your husband own the bakery yourselves?"

The pretty baker smiled, "I have no time for wedded bliss, I'm afraid. My cat, Jasper, is all I need to keep me happy. He's a great listener."

I understood her feline devotion. "I'm a cat lover, too. Mine's more of a talker, though."

Ava looked around the quaint shop. "Owning your own business is quite an accomplishment for a young woman on her own."

"Well, thank you," she said, "Now, have you made up your minds or do you need a few samples to narrow it down?"

Ava didn't peer down at the scrumptious treats again. She looked directly at Betty Smith. "I'd like to know how a woman could afford to open her own bakery after being fired from a good job in a private club."

The same question crossed my mind, but I had been trying to devise a more discreet way to ask.

Betty Smith's smile faded and her brow furrowed. "Who are you and what do you want?"

I felt like she deserved a direct answer. "I assume you heard about the death of Charles Whitmore. We are trying to find out who killed him."

She wiped her bangs off her face with the back of her hand. "I read that his wife did so you're a little late." Then she paused. "Wait—are you trying to find someone else to accuse? Is that why you came looking for me?"

I put my hands up defensively. "We didn't come to accuse you, we came to find out about your experience with him. We heard it wasn't a pleasant one and that it cost you your job," I explained.

She approached the counter, a little more relaxed. "I lost my job but that wasn't the worst part. That horrible experience left me with nightmares, if you really want to know. But I wouldn't kill the man. I got my revenge and you're looking at it. How do you think I got the money for this bakery?"

"I don't understand," I said.

"Me neither," Ava agreed.

Betty smoothed her hair back with both hands. "That animal attacked me after drinking a bottle of whiskey at the bar in the club one night a few years back. He had hit

on me before but I always turned him down. Most of the
girls who worked at the club thought he was handsome
and funny. They thought I should be flattered. I wasn't. I
told him he was a pig. It seemed to anger him that a
woman didn't appreciative his two-cent charm. He was
drunk and his anger turned physical. Afterward, the club
wanted to sweep the incident under the rug. But I was
roughed up and angry. So they gave me a few months'
pay and said they didn't need me anymore."

I was appalled. "That's awful." I could see by Ava's
expression she felt the same way. "What did you do?"

"I found out where he worked and went to his office.
I waited until he was there alone. I told him I wouldn't go
away until he gave me some money. At first, he brushed
me off. But I had nothing left to lose so I was persistent. I
gave him a deadline and began a countdown of the number of days until I swore I would turn his life upside
down with scandal and embarrassment. I told him I
would start with his personal life. That I knew who his
wife was and I wasn't afraid to tell her the truth. He got
scared. The pompous, rich lawyer was nothing more than
a cowardly weasel. In the end, he paid me every penny I
demanded. So you see, my revenge was much more satis-
fying than killing him. What would that have gotten me?"

Ava pressed her. "Maybe you couldn't let it go."

"I wasn't lying when I said I'm living my dream. I
have a great business, I make a decent living, and I answer to no one," Betty said, "I would never jeopardize

what I got—what I deserved from that awful man for the pain he put me through."

I believed her. "Any thoughts on who might've killed him?"

"I won't waste my energy thinking of him in life or death. I can't offer you any more than I've shared. All I can tell you is, without a doubt, the world is better off without Charles Whitmore."

I had to admit it was hard to argue with her last comment if the story she told us about Charles was true.

She placed her hands on top of the counter. "Do you have any more questions or can I get on with my day? I don't like talking about the past much these days. I focus on the day ahead and what it could bring. I believe I paid my dues with God, and He's allowed me a quiet and comfortable life."

"We appreciate your candor," I said, truthfully.

She shrugged. "I don't mind speaking the truth because I'm not ashamed of what I did. When no one else would help me, I had to help myself."

Ava placed her hands over Betty's. "You're a brave young woman. Keep looking ahead."

She looked appreciatively at Ava than me. "Your friend, Mrs. Whitmore, shouldn't feel bad for being duped by that man—everyone was. I just happen to have a good intuition for drunk men with anger problems. Besides, from what I saw, Mr. Whitmore's dark side rarely came out. It took an abundance of whiskey and a sense of indignation. I mean, he really thought that I should be flattered and excited to be with him. When he realized I wasn't, he snapped."

I shuddered. We thanked Betty again for talking to us and giving us some important insight into a side of Charles we luckily never knew. Ava and I were quiet as we walked to the car.

I glanced at Ava. "I'm having a hard time comprehending what we just heard."

"I'm at a loss for words," Ava agreed.

I stopped walking. "I don't think I would've put much stock into what she told us if we hadn't heard something eerily similar last night. It's weird. Here are two people accusing our long-time friend of the most despicable and disparaging behavior, yet I find myself believing them."

"Me too," Ava said, "There was an honesty and frankness about Betty, in particular, that made me trust her."

"Do we need to tell Mary about this?"

"Yes, but look on the bright side—" she began.

I looked at her as if she was insane. "What bright side?"

"It'll make her period of mourning considerably shorter," she said dryly.

She may have had a point.

Chapter 21

Ava and I went down to the pier where we were supposed to meet Jo. We arrived early. We figured there'd be time to go for a long walk along the shore but, to our surprise, Jo was already there. She looked upset. We walked quickly to meet her.

Ava greeted her with a sisterly hug. "What's wrong, my dear? You look perfectly bothered."

"I'm bothered all right," Jo began, "The people at that club were terrible!"

"What happened?" I asked.

Tears of frustration sat in her eyes. "Charles and Mary are among the most popular couples at the club. Everyone knows them and wants to be their friend. When I walked in today, many of those same people pretended not to recognize me or just whispered as I walked by."

Ava smoothed back Jo's hair in an effort to calm her. "Are you sure people recognized you?"

She aggressively pushed the tears away that escaped down her face. "Yes. I spent a lot of time there and Mary was always by my side then like a protective mother bear. She knew I was nervous around new people so she went out of her way to introduce me around, telling people I was her younger cousin, and she always included me in conversations. A lot of those same people pretended not to even see me."

I chewed on my thumbnail. "I wondered if that would happen, Jo. I don't think it's necessarily that they're turning their backs on you or Mary. Maybe they just don't know what to say or how to react. Uncomfortable situations can make people behave poorly."

Ava frowned at the excuses I proposed. "Would it be too difficult to ask how she or, at least, how Mary is doing? Could people be so paralyzed to forget proper social etiquette or to extend their sympathies?"

I shook my head. "Let's not write everyone off just yet. I don't want to assume they're all cold and uncaring. I have a feeling once a conversation is started, most of those people would offer their support."

Ava rolled her eyes. "You're such an optimist. It annoys me."

Jo seemed a little comforted by my words. "I guess I wasn't exactly friendly myself. I didn't really know who to talk to or what to say either."

Ava made a sweeping gesture with her arm. "Don't worry, my dear. We need to fill you in about our morning, too. With what we've learned about Charles's character, I can't say there'll be much written on his headstone."

Jo looked worried. "I'm almost scared to know."

I pressed my lips together. "Keep in mind we haven't spoken to his friends and supporters yet. Up until now, we've only been looking for those who might want to hurt him."

Ava looked at me sideways. "Isn't that the point?"

"Yes, but I think it's important to talk to people he liked and trusted, too. Charles was a complicated man. I think it'll help us get a better idea of where Charles's focus was these days."

Ava looked skeptical. "And you think his golf buddies will know?"

I nodded. "From what Erica told me, the men he golfed with were his closest friends. They might know more than you would expect. It sounds like golf was more than just a way to get some fresh air and exercise for Charles."

Ava sighed. "All right, let's see what we can find out. If nothing else, I could use a shot of whiskey."

I wagged my finger at her. "Please tell me you're joking."

"Izzy, it's a way to fit in," she stated. "I'm strategizing. I think it'll get us some respect, as long as we don't ask for an umbrella in our drink. We don't want to make spectacles of ourselves again."

I wasn't sure whether she was pulling my leg or not but I didn't really care. She was going along with the plan without any further complaint and that was worth keeping any thoughts I had on her so-called strategy to myself.

Jo was in no mood to return to the club so, after we stopped for lunch, we dropped her off at the police station to visit Mary. Then Ava and I headed back. If Erica was right about her timing, we would arrive just before tee off. I kept my fingers crossed.

It was a scorcher of a day. We parked the car and walked into the club. It seemed quiet until we headed to the back where the men's lounge was. It was packed. A lot of the men paused their conversations to look at us and make sure we weren't there for them. I imagine this would be a place a wife might instinctively know to come if her member-husband was late for dinner or some other expected event. I inquired with the staff who Charles normally played with and we were led to a group of three gentlemen sitting with what looked to be snifters of whiskey or rye. So far, this was just as Erica described. They ceased all talk when we approached.

"Good afternoon, gentlemen," I began.

"Good afternoon," the first man said a little appre-hensively.

The other two looked at each other and mumbled hello.

Ava was clearly irritated by the unfriendly greeting. It was not the typical reaction she received from men. "You can relax, fellas. We're not here to arrest you."

I immediately regretted bringing her and tried to smile through my annoyance. "My friend here is attempting to be funny. My name is Isabelle Walsh. This is Ava Russell."

"Is there something we can help you with?" the first gentleman asked.

I smiled at him. "Well, I hope so. You see, we're friends of Mary Whitmore."

The same gentlemen stood up and introduced himself and his two companions. He was tall and slender, probably in his mid-forties. His name was Harold Connors, Maggie Connors's husband, I noted. Next to him sat a short, bright-eyed man named Roger Adams, and the third man sitting across from Roger was an older-looking quiet man named Stanley Halloway.

"We were hoping to talk to you about Charles," I continued. "I understand you three were quite close to him?"

Harold hesitated. "I guess you could say we were close. We met regularly to play golf and enjoy an occasional glass of spirits."

Mr. Adams leaned in. "It's a terrible business what happened to Charles. We're all shocked and saddened by his passing."

I nodded my head. "As are we, of course. Ava and I

are trying to get a sense of what he meant to his friends to try and comfort Mary. She's having a hard time coming to terms with what's happened."

The third man, Stanley Halloway, cleared his throat. "Coming to terms with murdering her husband or coming to terms with being caught for it?" With that, he stood up abruptly and walked over to the bar.

Mr. Connors looked at us and sighed. "Please come and sit down. Don't mind Stanley. This has been very difficult for him. He's having a hard time accepting the loss of our friend."

Ava and I took a seat. "Mary is innocent," I said. "We are trying to find out who else may have had a motive to commit such a terrible act against Charles."

"One of the downfalls of being a lawyer is that people sometimes don't like you," Mr. Connors said. "In Charles's case, he had a personality that seemed to polarize people on top of that. You love him or you hate him. We were, of course, on the side of thinking the world of him. Charles was witty, smart, educated, and fun. But he was also brash, unapologetic, and outspoken,"

I sensed we had very limited time with our audience. "Of the people you know who did not like him, is there anyone who might hate him enough to kill him?"

Mr. Connors tapped his lips thoughtfully. "I think that a person has to have something in their nature to kill someone in cold blood. For example, no matter how much I hated someone, no matter what they had done to me or against me, I don't think I'd ever actually be able to commit the act of murder. While there are lots of people who might've thoroughly hated poor Charles, murder is more difficult to assess. With that being said, my answer is no, I really don't."

Ava looked him over. "You sound very confident in your assessment of the human mind."

"I am a criminal lawyer, Mrs. Russell. I've seen a lot of the ugly side of mankind," he answered.

I considered my next question. "What about his partner, William Stormwell? Do you think he could be capable?"

It looked like Mr. Connors pondered the question. "Hmm, I haven't spent much time with him. He seems a little reserved and spiritless to carry out such a bold act, wouldn't you say?"

"I hardly know Mr. Stormwell," I answered.

Ava turned to Mr. Connors. "Is it me or do you hold a certain respect for the killer?"

"Mrs. Russell, I just find it interesting that whoever killed Charles didn't seem to hesitate in doing so. You see, when someone is killed in a stabbing, there is often what is known as hesitation marks: one or two shallow wounds made before the deeper wounds responsible for the death. In Charles's case, there were no such markings. Whoever killed him did so with no reservation. It's a rare quality and one I find fascinating."

I was confused. "How do you know such specific details about what happened?"

"Oh, you two are not the first visitors we've had this afternoon. Detective Jones was here not long ago. He asked us a number of questions and we, in turn, asked him some. He was quite open about the scene of the crime and the circumstances surrounding Charles at the time of his death. In fact, we have been discussing it since he left."

I hoped they would expand. "So, you think that having no partial stab wounds is a significant clue?"

"Most definitely. One that may help Mary's case, in fact," he told us.

Ava and I looked at each other hopefully.

Mr. Connors saw our exchange. "Let me explain by way of example. Have you ladies heard of the Christmas Truce?"

We both shook our heads.

"During WWI there was a brief pause of fighting on the Western front in 1914. It lasted mostly from Christmas Eve to Christmas Day. Soldiers from both sides put down their weapons and came together to play football and share a few other social activities. You see the weaponry in that war forced them to fight in close proximity. They'd often be only thirty to seventy yards apart. So when Christmas arrived, both sides weary and wanting a break for the holiday, soldiers stopped fighting and began to visit across enemy lines and exchange gifts like food and tobacco. It was a chance for the men to see a more human side of their enemies. But it was not good in terms of the war, because many soldiers found it hard to get back to killing each other. They had seen a side they could relate to, not the propaganda-laden image they had been shown. The superior officers saw it as a mistake and never repeated it. WWII didn't have such problems because they were never close enough to relate to one another. The further distance makes it easier to kill because it allows for a greater psychological and emotional separation," he finished.

Mr. Adams observed us as we listened intently to Mr. Connors. "As you can see, Harold is used to speaking to a jury. He has a flair for the dramatic and likes to hear himself talk. It's the nature of the business."

Mr. Connors ignored his friend. "My point is that your killer did not have the natural hesitation that usually comes with killing someone so close by. Whoever killed Charles did so with no emotion. I believe you are probably right in thinking Mary is innocent of the act. If it had been her, the crime would've been messier, bloodier."

I tried to smile appreciatively but I was so disturbed by the sheer gusto Mr. Connors used to speculate on Charles's murder, I guessed it didn't quite come out right. "We appreciate your support, Mr. Connors."

"Your welcome." He looked pleased with himself. "I wait with baited breath to learn the identity, if you, or the authorities, are ever able to determine who executed this masterful crime."

Ava looked unimpressed. "We'll keep your curiosity

as a renewed motivation to solve the crime."

He took no notice of her. "If I were a betting man, I would probably put my money on a professional killer: a murder-for-hire sort of situation."

My eyes widened. "Doesn't that seem a little far-fetched?"

His cavalier attitude persisted. "Perhaps. It's just a theory, take it or leave it."

My dislike of this man grew with each word he spoke but I was resolute to understand his callous game theory. "That precludes the first point you made: that Charles must've known the killer. Charles wouldn't have brought out a bottle of wine and invited someone he didn't know to sit and have a drink with him."

His eyes lit up with pleasure. "Excellent, Mrs. Walsh. That is what you need to bridge. There lies the true mystery of the case."

Mr. Connors became distracted by some boisterous newcomers who had jus entered the lounge. But as his attention waned, and he left our area to engage others in conversation, Mr. Adams sat up more attentively. It seemed he had just been waiting for his turn to speak. It would be hard to have anything other than a one-way conversation with Harold Connors, I imagined.

He had a much softer approach. "Ladies, I think you need to consider another point. There were a lot of big changes going on in Charles's life. That could be important in who you keep on your list of suspects."

I was interested to hear more. "What changes are you talking about, Mr. Adams?"

"For one thing, he was planning to leave his partnership with William Stormwell and take as many clients with him as he could. They had a troubled relationship and Charles was tired of him."

"Wouldn't that pose a big risk to his career, Mr. Adams?"

Mr. Adams gave us a deferential smile. "Mr. Stormwell is a good lawyer, but Charles felt confident he had the loyalty of many, if not most of their long-standing clients. It might've destroyed William's career but Charles would've landed on his feet."

"Any further insights?" I asked.

"Your friend, Mary, of course. She may have thought Charles didn't know of her recent activity. But this is small town. The wife of any prominent lawyer does not visit a divorce attorney without it getting out," he informed us. "Those were the most current issues in Charles's life that could incite tremendous passion, often the motivation for such a crime."

"What about Mr. Connors theory about no hesitation wounds?"

Mr. Adams paused. "I'll admit that does warrant consideration. However, I am convinced current events pose such strong motives that they must trump the importance of hesitation wounds or lack thereof. In this case, I would consider the timing a key factor."

I respected his insight. "We'll certainly keep that in mind."

Mr. Halloway wandered back over. He ignored us and reminded Mr. Adams that they had less than five minutes until tee off. We thanked Mr. Adams and proceeded to walk to the entrance. Mr. Connors gave us a holler and a wink from the bar as we left.

Ava shuddered when we got outside. "Is it me or did Mr. Connors seem to be getting some sort of amusement out of their friend's death?"

My eyes widened and I conceded. "Yes. But I've got an even more disturbing question."

"What's that?"

"How is such a lovely lady like Maggie Connors married to such a pompous ass?" I demanded.

She put her arm around my shoulders. "One mystery at a time, my dear."

Chapter 22

When we arrived at the police station, Jo was reading a magazine on an office chair tucked in a corner. I waved at her but I was anxious to talk to Mary so I requested a visit immediately. The patient officer on duty obliged my request one more time. When I entered the cell, Mary looked pleased to see me. She assured me that she was faring much better, and that she'd had a number of friends by to see her, as well as her lawyer. I sat down and decided the best way to approach our conversation was to be direct.

Mary apparently knew me well enough to see this wasn't going to be a pleasant conversation by looking at my face. "Izzy, let me have it. What have you found out? I can tell it won't be nice and I'm prepared to hear it."

"Mary—" I hesitated. "Mary, have you ever heard of the name Betty Smith?"

"No, I haven't. Is that someone Charles may have been involved with?" she asked.

"Not exactly. You see Miss Smith is a woman who says Charles assaulted her and that she blackmailed him, in return for a considerable amount of money."

She looked offended. "Charles had women falling all over him. Why would he attack someone?"

"According to Miss Smith, Charles had made some advances toward her which she, at first, lightly dismissed. But he was persistent and continued the unwanted attention for some time. The more she thwarted his advances, the more aggressive he became, culminating in the night of the alleged assault."

Mary stiffened and her complexion paled. "When did she claim this was?"

I sighed. "Some time ago, late one night at the club. She said he was intoxicated and saw her working alone in the kitchen. He came in and, once again, made a pass at her. She told him he was pathetic. She alleges this is when he became extremely angry and had his way with her."

Mary stared at the wall but I knew she heard every word I said.

"That's not the only woman claiming to have been assaulted by him," I informed her.

Her eyes remained focused on the wall and a single

tear fell on her cheek. "Charles had a dark side. It intensified after his brother died in the war. It was rarely triggered, mind you, but the story you're telling me is giving me shivers." She turned her head and looked into my eyes, "You see, Charles liked to get his way. Everyone does, of course, but with Charles, it was different. He didn't like people telling him no or denying him anything he felt he deserved, which translated into anything he wanted. With the charmed life he led, it was rarely an issue. He was popular, wealthy, and had no one to answer to. He also liked to be in control. These two things are similar but his need for control usually led him to keep himself in check, as well as others. Real trouble only materialized if he lost this control and was drinking heavily. You see, Charles often had a drink in his hand, but he very rarely became inebriated, at least in public."

"When he was at home he would change?" I asked her intently. "Did he ever hurt you?"

"Only once did I see a side of Charles that scared me. He didn't hurt me, but he came close. The very next day is when he ordered the renovation on the boathouse. We never discussed it but I knew that's why he did it. I also knew, when he was there, never to disturb him. It wasn't only his office, it was also a place where he could shut himself in and let go. The night he was murdered was the first time I had ever gone in, uninvited."

Our eyes met and I could see her fear. I didn't know what to say to comfort her. But now I could make sense of something that had been nagging me. Although I found the women we'd talked to mostly sincere and believable, I couldn't bridge how Jo, having lived with Mary and Charles for a year, could never have seen the darker side of Charles. Now I could. Most people couldn't afford a place to hide their demons so completely. It made me wonder how often he chose to escape into his drunken alter ego and, if it was that aggressive, angry side, that his killer encountered the night of his death. Our conversation was cut short when a police officer came in and told me our time was up.

As I was leaving, I saw Detective Jones. He asked me to sit down for a few minutes. I obliged, of course.

He fixed me a cup of coffee then sat down. "I wanted to ask you how your detecting was going."

"I'm learning a lot more about Charles than I ever knew. It has certainly opened up a range of people who probably shed no tears upon his death," I admitted.

His brows furrowed. "I'm impressed at your instincts so far. Mind sharing your thoughts?"

"Thank you, Detective. May I inquire why you're asking me?"

A slight smile emerged on his rugged face. "I've got good news for you. I'm going to let Mary Whitmore go."

A feeling of relief surged through my body. "Detective Jones, that's wonderful news. Does Mary know?"

"Not yet. I've just come back from the morgue where the autopsy has been concluded. Based on the findings, there's no way I could see Mrs. Whitmore physically capable of committing this crime."

It's finally over, I thought.

As if he read my mind, Detective Jones cautioned me, "I'm not officially stating your friend is innocent. I may be back with more questions. I can't be sure at this point she didn't get help to commit an act she wasn't able to do herself."

"Are you suggesting that she may have had someone else kill Charles for her?"

He leaned forward in his chair. "There are certain specifics surrounding how Charles died that suggest it could've been a job as opposed to a crime of passion."

"Ah yes, Mr. Connors's theory, no hesitation wounds," I surmised.

He glanced at me with, what I believed, was respect. "Yes, it's in the realm of possibilities. But that's not the only detail. The stab wound is so deep, it must've been carried out by someone with considerable strength and skill."

"If that were the case, and Mary was suspected of murder-for-hire, she would face an even tougher penalty if found guilty."

"Absolutely. First-degree murder, in fact," Detective Jones informed me.

My heart sank once again. "You certainly know how to dampen good news."

"I'm just letting you know the facts, Mrs. Walsh. I wouldn't pop open the bubbly just yet."

"I'll keep that in mind," I said soberly.

"Mrs. Walsh, you can bring your friend home. That's something you can feel good about. I'm sure she'll appreciate that, even if it is just temporary."

"Yes, sir."

Within an hour, they released Mary. We took her home. She showered while Mrs. Collins made delicious roast pork. Mary, Jo, Ava, and I ate heartily. It felt like it had been ages since we had been able to all sit down together. Mary was exhausted. After a glass of wine following the early dinner, she went straight to bed. Jo stayed to make sure she'd be there when Mary woke up. Ava figured it would be a good time to check in at home. I needed some time to think. I called Frank and updated him. He told me there was no need to rush back and that he and the kids were keeping busy. So after dropping Ava off, instead of heading home, I went to the harbor.

Some people needed a quiet, peaceful environment in order to concentrate, but sometimes I preferred some hustle and bustle. It seemed to inspire my mind to keep moving. The sun was still high in the sky despite the evening hour, and I knew there would still be a lot of people enjoying the lovely summer weather. I parked my car and went into the popular Oceanside Marketeria to grab a coffee. I emerged five minutes later with a double scoop of vanilla ice cream—the coffee looked stale. I planted myself on a bench outside the store and tried to eat my treat before the sun melted it all over my skirt. I was losing the battle in a most undignified manner.

From where I was sitting, I could see a lot of boats in the harbor and just a glimpse of the beach. It looked busy still, with families sitting around on blankets and kids running around in what looked to be a big game of tag. I smiled at the picturesque scene before me. Then an idea occurred to me. I wandered down to where some of the sailboats were docked and began to read the names. It was about the fifth boat I looked at when I hit a bout of luck. Bobbing in the water sat a pristine boat called *Sharon's Beauty*. I was standing on the dock admiring it when a man walked up on the deck from below. It was not the picture I had in mind of a jealous husband. In front of me stood the epitome of the type of man so many women swoon for: tall, blond, and handsome.

"Donald Wright?" I hollered up.

He looked down at me curiously. "Yes?"

"Do you have a few minutes to talk? It's important."

"Who are you?" he asked kindly.

"My name is Isabelle Walsh. I won't keep you long, promise."

He stopped what he was doing and looked me over. "I was just getting ready to go out on the water for a quick evening sail. What is it I can help you with?"

"I have a few questions for you regarding Charles Whitmore," I said plainly.

"Give me a minute," he said and hopped down off his boat coming face to face with me. He had an easy, natural smile. "Now, why is it that people always re-member the worst things about a person?"

I was caught off guard—not only because of the question but his blue eyes were almost piercing. "Excuse me?"

"I'm guessing you are looking for people who had problems with Charles?"

"Yes, I suppose that's true," I admitted.

"And what is your interest in that whole mess, Miss Walsh?"

"It's Mrs. Walsh and by *that whole mess* do you mean Charles's death?" It bothered me the way he characterized the murder.

"Yes, I do. Charles created so many messes it would be good to clarify," he commented dryly. "So, what's your interest in his death?"

"I'm a friend of Mary Whitmore's."

He inspected me. "So you are looking for suspects to shift the focus off your friend."

"I wouldn't quite characterize it like that, no. In case you hadn't heard, Mary was released," I said flustered, "I was nearby the dock and thought I'd stop by to see if you had any thoughts or feelings about him that you would be willing to share."

"My problems with Charles were in the past. We certainly weren't close at the time of his death, nor were we ever, but the only feeling I could say I had for Charles before his death was gratitude," he said, still looking at me, a more serious demeanor setting in.

"I don't understand."

"I will explain this to you quickly because I want to get back to my day. I assume I'll only be able to accomplish that if you're satisfied with my answer," he said.

I didn't argue the point.

"My wife, Sharon, and I are closer than we've ever been because of Charles. I'm sure you've been made aware of a mutual dislike Charles and I had of one another but if it weren't for him, I don't know if my wife and I would be as happy as we are now."

"How so?" I asked.

"You see, several months ago, Sharon and Charles were part of a committee organizing a charity golf tournament. She was reluctant to join but I pushed her into it, thinking it would be a good way for her to make a few friends at the club, as she is naturally a little shy and introverted. Charles was in charge of the event and seemed to take a special interest in my wife. The two of them started talking a lot more, and that got others at the club talking too, just not about the tournament. At first, I barely noticed. Men paying attention to my wife was not something new. I was also a little more self-involved than I'd like to admit. I'm afraid my hobbies, golf and sailing, were getting more attention than my wife. I spent my free time either on the golf course or at the pier. I didn't even notice that my wife had found a way to make up for the attention she was missing at home—"

I interrupted. "Are you telling me that you're grateful Charles had an affair with you wife?"

His blue eyes turned icy. "You've got it all wrong, Mrs. Walsh. Let me explain something to you so you understand the truth about Charles and Sharon's relationship."

"Please do," I encouraged him.

"Sharon was angry with me. She was fed up of feeling invisible. When Charles started focusing his smooth charm on her, she felt flattered and enjoyed the attention he showered her with. But that's where it ended. At first, when I saw or, I should say, paid attention to what was happening, I went crazy with anger and jealousy. I didn't know what to do. I confronted Sharon and said things to her I wish I hadn't. But then she turned it around on me. She told me of her loneliness and unhappiness in our marriage. I was shocked. We were high school sweethearts. I'd only ever loved her and she me. But I had taken her for granted. Not paid attention to her needs. Believe me, I changed all that. Since that time, our marriage has never been better. I won't let that happen again."

"So how do you know that Sharon and Charles didn't have an affair?" I asked.

"Because I trust my wife."

"Did you trust Charles?" I asked.

"I didn't need to, Mrs. Walsh. A good marriage is founded on love and respect. Trust is an integral part of that. My wife and I have it in spades," he said proudly.

"And Charles?"

"Charles was very different from me. I'm more quiet

and reserved, whereas he was outgoing and flamboyant. I was an easy target for him. He knew he could get under my skin and he enjoyed it. He liked to tease me and make jokes at my expense. Sometimes it got to me and I got angry. Can you blame me?"

"So why would he do it?" I asked, puzzled.

"People never let go of the rumors about Charles and my wife and, in turn, they were always curious to see the interaction between Charles and myself. I think he liked the drama and the attention."

"Didn't that bother you?"

"Sure it did, but I still I have a lot of friends at the club and I enjoy going there. One man is not going to dictate where I go and don't go. I just have to put up with it once in a while. I'll admit I won't be mourning Charles, but I still think it's awful what happened."

"One last question: Did you call Charles's office and threaten to hurt him a few weeks ago?" I asked.

He looked a little taken aback. "I did call, yes, but the word *threaten* is hardly accurate. I was angered by Charles's antics at the club regarding my wife and I wanted him to back off."

"What did he do to provoke the phone call?" I asked.

He sighed. "What he always does: singled her out and embarrassed her in front of other people."

"How did he do that?" I pressed.

"He walked by her, winked, and said hello."

"Such a small gesture prompted you to call and threaten him at work?" I asked.

"You're not getting it. It was all a game to him. These little gestures hurt my wife and got people talking, wondering, and gossiping. She tried to distance herself from him but he got a kick out of her reaction: she blushed in shame then came to me in tears. It wasn't right. I called his office because I wanted to meet him face to face, without other people watching, to demand he stop ridiculing my wife and let it go."

"And when did you have your *tete-a-tete*?"

"I never had a chance to. I thought about going to see him last weekend at his house but something came up and I never went. Two days later I found out he was dead."

"So the very weekend you planned on confronting him, he was murdered," I concluded.

"The irony is not lost on me, Mrs. Walsh."

"The irony or the convenience?"

"Mr. Whitmore played games with people. It often entertained those around him and made people laugh. But not everyone was laughing. There was a dark side to him, maybe one that you never saw. But he liked to know people's weaknesses, their vulnerabilities. He played on them. He was a great manipulator and used people's trust and secrets to amuse himself. My guess is that he pushed someone too far. But you're looking at the wrong man, Mrs. Walsh. Now, may I please go? I promised my wife I wouldn't be late so that just leaves me a short time to get out on the water before I have to be home."

I looked at him intently. "Yes, Mr. Wright. Enjoy

your afternoon. Thank you for taking time to talk to me."

"You're welcome, Mrs. Walsh. I hope you find the answers you're looking for," he said. With that, he shook my hand cordially and hopped back onto his boat.

Chapter 23

I decided to pay a visit to Sharon Wright on my way home. With the conversation between Donald Wright and me so fresh in my mind, I figured it was a good time. I wanted to see if she could confirm what her husband told me. It took a bit of help to find out where they lived, but luckily I called Maggie Connors and she was able to quickly find out the Wright's address. I pulled up to the house and got out. It was a large home with a beautiful garden to match. Colorful flowers lined the walkway leading up to the door and I took a moment to smell them. Every year I meant to put more time into my garden and, as of yet, it hadn't happened.

I approached the door and knocked. A moment later

Sharon opened the door, looking surprised. "Isabelle!"

"Hi, Sharon, you looked so upset yesterday when you left, I wanted to come by and see if you were okay," I said.

"That's very thoughtful of you," she said with a cautious smile. "How did you know where to find me?"

"I just asked at the club and they told me."

"Of course. I'm fine, Isabelle, thank you for your concern. Would you like to come in for a minute? You can try my homemade lemonade. I just made a fresh jug,"

"Sounds delicious. I love lemonade."

I went in and sat at the kitchen table while Sharon poured our drinks. It still smelled like fresh cut lemons. I looked around and noted what a stylish, yet comfortable, home she and Donald had.

Sharon sat down next to me. Up close, she was just as pretty as when I first met her at the club. Although she was much more casually dressed and wearing no makeup, her delicate features and light green eyes gave her a natural beauty that I could see would get the attention of any man.

"I hope I'm not keeping you from anything?"

"Not at all. Donald is out on the water and I'm just puttering around the house," she replied cheerily.

"Great, I won't keep you long."

"No problem. I have dinner all made and that was about all I had to get done today. It's staying warm in the oven so I can relax." She smiled, looking quizzically at me. "I get the impression you didn't just come by to see how I'm feeling." .

"I wanted to ask you about someone from the club."

"As I told you, I mostly keep to myself. I really don't know anyone there well," she admitted.

"I'm pretty sure you know him," I said lightly.

"Who is it?" she asked curiously.

"Charles Whitmore."

She frowned. "Why are you asking *me* about Charles?"

"I heard you two were…close."

"What are you implying? And what business is it of yours?" she said, looking angry and confused.

"Look, Sharon, I'm just trying to find out the truth about what happened to Charles."

"The *truth* is that I have no idea what happened to him," she stated.

"I'm not suggesting that you did. But I was told you were close to him not that long ago, so I thought you might have some thoughts on it."

"Charles befriended me when we first moved here. I thought he was kind and funny…" she said.

"And handsome?" I asked.

"I love my husband and assumed, wrongly, I now know, that marriage was respected by people around here as much as it was by me. I'll admit I was flattered that Charles took an interest in me but I would never betray my husband—by thought or action. I took my vows for life," she attested.

"And what about Charles?"

A dark cloud seemed to loom over his pretty features. "I don't think he had respect for anything."

"What happened that changed your mind about him?"

She cleared her throat and held her head up stiffly. "He humiliated me."

"By making a pass at you?"

Before Sharon could answer, Donald walked in. He didn't look nearly as relaxed as he had earlier in the day.

He was glaring at me. "What are you doing here?"

"I just wanted to ask Sharon a few questions."

"I think you've asked enough questions for today," he growled.

Sharon looked confused. "What are you two talking about?"

He looked at me, "I guess you didn't expect I'd be home so soon? Luckily, I decided to skip the sail for today after our little chat ruined my mood."

He then turned to his wife. "Didn't Miss Walsh here mention that she'd already talked to me today? Let me be more specific, that she already *grilled* me today?"

"No," Sharon said, "I don't understand."

"Our guest is a friend of Mary Whitmore's. Mrs. Whitmore is currently under suspicion for killing her husband so Miss. Walsh is trying to find someone else to pin it on," he explained, "Looks like you and I are on the short list."

"Is that true?" Sharon demanded, looking at me.

"Mary *is* a close friend of mine. And *I am* trying to help her, but I'm not trying to 'pin it' on anyone. I'm just trying to find out the truth."

"Here's some truth for you, Mrs. Walsh," he said bitterly. "Charles Whitmore took advantage of the good nature of my wife. He preyed on her shy manner and thought he could get away with it because he has an enormous ego. I was patient and answered all your questions honestly. But you've crossed the line harassing and baiting my wife."

I stood back. "I'm sorry, that is not my intention. Now please tell me, what do you mean when you said he thought he could '*get away with it*'? Did Charles hurt you, Sharon?"

"Don't talk to this meddling woman, Sharon. We can't trust her," Donald instructed.

"Donald, maybe we should—" Sharon said calmly.

"No, Sharon. You don't need to be scared anymore. The bastard is dead," he said in the most soothing manner he could muster. Then he looked at me fiercely. "I want you out of our house. And I mean now!"

I watched Donald. "Did you make sure that Charles couldn't hurt Sharon anymore?"

He met my gaze defiantly. "You listen to me: I didn't kill him but I would gladly shake the hand of the man that did."

"Donald, it's okay, you said it. He can't hurt us anymore," Sharon said trying to calm her husband. She then turned to me, "It's time for you to leave. Do not come back here again."

I was out the door and into my car before the shock of what just happened set in. Donald Wright behaved like a completely different person than the one I met earlier today. No doubt, it was because he didn't like me talking to Sharon. But if he was so protective of his wife that even a few questions would set him off, how would he have reacted if Charles hurt her more than with just words?

I drove away with my heart beating wildly. I wanted nothing more than to go home and forget this mess. But I resolved not to worry Frank any more so I went back to Mary's. When I got there, Mary and Jo were sitting out by the cliff, looking pensively over the ocean. I decided not to disturb them, especially with the way I was feeling. Instead, I walked quietly toward the door, where Mrs. Collins greeted me as I opened it. She could see I was upset.

"Dear Lord, what now?" she asked.

Considering my friend had just been released from jail, she was understandably confused and worried by my obvious distress.

"It's nothing Mrs. Collins, I just think the last few days are catching up with me," I said somewhat truthfully.

"As they are with everyone around here. Go straight

upstairs and have a lie down. It'll do you a world of good to let your mind and body settle," she said soothingly, "I'll even make you a fresh pot of coffee for when you wake up."

"Thank you, Mrs. Collins." I followed her instruction and slowly climbed the stairs toward my room. I needed to shake off my nerves and knew a few minutes of peace and quiet could accomplish it.

I laid down and closed my eyes. When I got up, I felt a bit confused but much calmer. A splash of water on my face refreshed me instantly. As I headed back downstairs, I wasn't sure how long I'd been sleeping. I peered out a window and saw the sun hadn't fully set so I figured it was still a reasonable hour. Voices were talking quietly nearby. I recognized Jo and Mary's voice but wasn't sure about the other one until I walked into the living room and saw Erica sitting across from Mary.

Mary smiled warmly, looking worlds better than she did this morning. "Izzy, are you all right? I think Mrs. Collins is concerned about you."

"I'm fine, thank you. It's just been a few long days, as you obviously know. I suppose it caught up with me." I wasn't ready to mention my run in with Donald Wright, especially since I still wasn't sure what to make of it so I just sat down and joined my friends quietly.

A moment later, Mrs. Collins entered the room like a vision, holding a tray complete with tea, milk, sugar, and a few cookies. She wouldn't even let me get up, insisting on preparing my cup and bringing it right to me. I thanked her gratefully. She left the room promptly and our conversation continued. It turned out that, while I was napping, Erica came by to return some of Charles's personal possessions from the office.

She seemed thrilled to find Mary home. "I knew the police would let Mary go. With nothing more than a marital spat after a little wine, they had absolutely no evidence to make the charges stick. But I'm relieved she's home so soon."

"You'll get no argument from me there," Mary stated. "Izzy, we were just talking about going for a walk in the garden before it's too dark. Why don't you join us?"

I scarfed down the coffee and agreed to go with them on an evening stroll. The four of us left the house together. It was finally beginning to cool down so I excused myself to get a sweater from the car. I was grabbing it from the front seat when something caught my eye. There was a torn note tucked under my windshield wiper. Odd. I unfolded the plain white paper. An involuntary cry of fear escaped my lips as I read it. I looked up and saw Jo, Mary, and Erica rushing to my side.

"Izzy!" Jo shouted, running over.

"What is it? What's wrong?" Mary cried, she and Erica not far behind.

I was certain they could see the fright in my eyes.

I handed Mary the scribbled, torn note, and she, Jo, and Erica huddled together to read it.

You will die next if you don't stop meddling.

Mary turned white and looked terrified. Jo grabbed my hand and looked around frantically.

Erica looked shocked but put a firm hand on my shoulder in an effort to soothe my nerves, "You're okay, Isabelle. Someone is just trying to scare you." She held my gaze. "Take a deep breath."

I followed Erica's instructions and reread the note. Something about it wasn't making sense to me, but I couldn't quite put my finger on what.

"There is a maniac out there!" Mary said exasperated.

"Or there's a maniac right here," I whispered.

"What do you mean?" Erica asked.

Jo clapped her hands over her cheeks. "Whoever left her that note must've done so while Izzy was lying down. He was *just here* while the four of us were inside feeling safe."

"Dear God, you're right!" Mary cried.

"That *is* an unsettling thought," Erica agreed. "Let's get back inside and call Detective Jones."

Within half an hour, Mary's house was once again crawling with police. Yet another long night ensued. Ava returned as soon as we called her and told her about the note. I called Frank and told him what happened. He wanted to come, too, but I explained how many officers were here and told him I didn't want the children to be frightened. He reluctantly agreed to stay put. Police detail was assigned to guard the house and premises. After telling Detective Jones and my friends what happened with the Wrights, he wanted to know in detail everywhere else we'd been and who else we'd seen in the last few days.

He looked concerned. "You've certainly been busy." Although he'd warned us to keep out of trouble, he was courteous enough not to bring it up now that we had put ourselves in harm's way.

Under the safe guard of the police, I thought I'd try to get a good night's sleep. Even though it hadn't been long since I'd awoken from my nap, I was feeling drained, body and mind. Luckily, Detective Jones agreed. He told us he'd be in and out of Mary's while investigating but would return tomorrow afternoon regardless of his findings to properly check up on us. In the meantime, he told us to stick together and stay close by. I barely remember getting ready for bed. I slept like a rock.

When I woke up in the morning, Ava was already in the shower. I quickly called Frank to bid him a good morning from the bedroom telephone and thank him again for his love and patience. He told me he missed me. It was good to hear. I promised to be home by the end of the day. When I got off the phone, I could hear lots of activity going on downstairs, but I kept turning over in bed. All I could think about was the threatening note left for me. Something about it was nagging me. I felt like some obscure part of my brain recognized something that had not yet connected to the rest of it. But as I went over it again and again in my head, I just got frustrated. There was only one thing I could think of to do: I needed to get to the library. It was quiet there and I needed to think without any distractions or interruptions.

But it wasn't as easy as getting in my car and driving away. Since finding the note, the police requested that we stay put. But I knew we were close to the truth, and I wanted to find it before the murderer found us. I tried to reason with the officers stationed at Mary's house, but they were uncomfortable about the notion of me going out on my own. I decided to call Detective Jones. I explained my frustration and requested a day pass. He saw no humor in my feeble attempt at a joke but gave his consent for a library visit if I brought a friend along and returned before noon. I agreed to his terms and dragged Ava with me.

She wrinkled her nose. "I don't understand why we have to go to the library."

"I think I'm having déjà vu from high school," I said dryly.

"We don't even know what we're looking for. What does going to the library have to do with finding the killer?"

I had explained my reasoning three or four times but she must not have heard me. "I need a quiet place to think."

"Fine. I've always found the atmosphere in the library a bit stifling but you know me, I'm a good sport. I trust your intuition," she said proudly.

Two hours later, Ava was pacing the aisles of books and I was left with no answers. I had scoured through some books, read all the recent magazines, and sat quietly staring at the ceiling for what felt like days. Still nothing.

I now knew how Ava felt whenever I brought her here. "All right, we can go now."

"Are you sure?" she asked cautiously.

"Yes, I think we've been here long enough. I thought being in a quiet space surrounded by inspiring authors would somehow trigger what's been nagging me but I've racked my brain and still gotten nowhere," I admitted.

She paused. "I know a place that would inspire deep thoughts."

"Where?" I demanded.

She pointed to a poster on the wall, "Not bad, huh?"

"Whoa," is all I got out.

There in front of us was a big poster with a photograph of an elaborate garden surrounding a bridge over a pond. Next to, it was a famous Monet painting which echoed the scene.

"I bet that's the place Erica was telling us about. What was it called?" I asked.

"Giverny," Ava remembered.

The large poster of the garden next to the painting that captured it was part of a library display showing highlights of France. Wineries, castles, and beaches around France were pictured on the wall display.

"Pretty neat, isn't it," Ava said.

"Amazing." I took a minute to study the display before letting out a big sigh. "Hard to believe that dinner party was less than a week ago."

"C'mon, let's go," Ava said. As if sensing my defeat, she put her arm around my shoulder affectionately and led me outside.

We walked out to the car and, in typical fashion, my car keys were hiding in my purse. I rummaged through it to find them and cursed under my breath as I realized I had inadvertently stolen a magazine from the library. I spun on my heel and waved it in the air at Ava, as an explanation for my change in direction.

"Thief!" Ava cried out loud. "All these years I thought I knew you. But now I see the truth." She shook her head in mock disappointment, put on her sunglasses, and leaned against the car, catching a few rays of sunshine while I sauntered back to the library entrance.

I glanced down at the magazine and immediately recognized the library was not where it needed to go. Sharon Wright had dropped it at the club. I had forgotten all about it. I wasn't sure if Sharon was done with it so I could pass it on to Erica or if she wanted to peruse it a little longer. I debated dropping it off.

Then it hit me. A cold sensation rushed through body and I couldn't move. I looked at the cover again and got into the car. I told Ava to do the same.

Ava knew by the look on my face not to ask questions. She sat quietly. I drove fast. In less than ten minutes, we pulled into a parking spot. I got out of the car and entered the door of the Twin Oaks Police Station. Ava was right behind me, although I barely noticed. Detective Jones was the first person I saw. I must've looked as shaken up as I felt, given his reaction when he saw me.

"Mrs. Walsh, Mrs. Russell, are you all right? Come sit down at my desk," he instructed without hesitation. He asked a colleague to get us each a glass of water. "What's going on?" he demanded.

"I know who did it," I whispered.

"Who did what?" he asked.

I tried to relax my nerves just long enough to get my words out clearly. "I know who killed Charles Whitmore."

Ava stared at me in disbelief. A police officer nonchalantly dropped off the water on the desk. Detective Jones passed a glass of it to me and began talking slowly, giving me clear instruction. "Have a drink and take a breath. You need to calm down before this conversation goes any further. I'd like to know what you have to say but if you faint now, and it looks like you're going to, then I'm going to have to wait longer, and I just don't have the patience for that." He smiled kindly and spoke to me in a soothing manner I wouldn't have thought him capable of.

Ava once again put her arm around my trembling shoulders. When she was scared, she got uncharacteristically quiet. This was one of those times. She hadn't said a word since the library, or maybe she had but I just didn't hear it. I took a drink of water and began to talk.

When I was done, Detective Jones looked at me thoughtfully. "Let's test your theory," was all he said.

He made a list of the people we needed to see and called each one with a mandatory meeting time for an hour away. Everyone was instructed to gather at the Whitmore's. He insisted Ava and I drive with him—he was still wary of my strength—and we headed out.

I had butterflies in my stomach as if I was going on stage for the opening night of a play. What made it different was that I didn't know the end of the script. It was time to find out.

Chapter 24

Mary and Jo were waiting for us at the house. It wasn't long before everyone else we'd called began to arrive. Donald and Sharon got there shortly after us. Donald was looking quite dismayed as he and Sharon came inside.

"I want to know what was so damned important we had to interrupt our meal and rush over here."

Detective Jones addressed him, "I'm going to require a little patience on your part, Mr. Wright."

Before Donald could argue, Betty Smith was shown into the sitting room with us and didn't look very pleased herself. "Whoever called this impromptu meeting is responsible for three batches of fresh tarts being ruined at my shop. This better be worth it." She looked around and glared at anyone who looked back.

Lastly, William and Erica arrived together. They were a little more amiable but no less confused. "Can someone please tell us what is going on here?" William said.

Detective Jones finally stepped forward. "Thank you all for coming here on such short notice. I am aware that none of you are happy about it, but I assure you it is well worth your while. You will understand shortly why the secrecy was so important. Everyone please take a seat. Mrs. Walsh is going to take over for me now. I need you all to listen to her with your full attention."

The butterflies returned but I was feeling a little calmer now. "I have to ask all of you some very personal questions. It is imperative you tell *all of us here* the truth. There is a reason why I am asking you these questions in front of each other. It is the only way I can get to the answers and explanations we need."

Donald glared at me impatiently. "Well, get on with it then."

"Okay, I will, thank you," I said. I looked at Betty and nodded. "I need to start with you first."

"Sure, pick on the single lady," she said, rolling her eyes. "I've been nothing but honest and straightforward with you Mrs. Walsh. What more do you want?"

"Nothing more, Betty. That is precisely why and how you fit into this. Please fill us in as to the nature of your relationship with Mr. Whitmore."

She looked around at the faces in the room. She then

paused and took in a deep breath. "But I'm not ashamed anymore," she began with a rebellious air. "Mr. Whitmore was a wolf in a nice suit. He played the suave gentleman but he was anything but. After a brief period of flattering comments and dopey gallantry, that scumbag forced himself on me. He thought he could get away with it because of the difference in our situations. So I…blackmailed …him." Betty paused and looked at the detective. "I mean I then *persuaded* him to give me some cash to start a bakery. In exchange, I swore not to tell his wife."

"Thank you for being so forthcoming, Betty. You're a brave woman," I said sincerely.

"Is that it? Or do you want me to wait and tell it to the six o'clock news?" she said sarcastically.

"That'll do just fine, thank you," I said.

No one else in the room made a sound. Donald was squeezing Sharon's hand firmly. William looked shocked but said nothing. All eyes were back on me.

"Following Miss Smith's account of her troubled relationship with Mr. Whitmore, I'd like to hear from Mr. and Mrs. Wright next," I said.

"We, too, have been honest and patient with you, Mrs. Walsh. What more do you want from us?" Donald said gruffly.

I shook my head. "I'm afraid I don't believe you, Donald. I think there is much you didn't share with me and now is the time to get it out."

"I don't know what you're talking about," he said.

I addressed Sharon. "Mrs. Wright, it is of the utmost importance that you tell us exactly what happened between you and Mr. Whitmore. You told me the other day that he began to pay extra attention to you and that he crossed the line, disrespecting your marriage. But you didn't explain the details of what happened."

"There's really nothing to tell," Sharon turned red and looked at Donald for help.

"Mr. Whitmore made a few passes at my wife, just as you suggested," Donald volunteered.

Detective Jones spoke up. "Mr. Wright I can take your wife down to the police station, if that would jog her memory better, and allow her to answer these questions on her own. Would that make it easier?"

"No, no, please," Sharon protested. "My husband is just trying to protect me. I don't want any more trouble. I will tell you what you want to know."

"Sharon—" Donald said.

"Donald, please. Let me speak. I just need to get it out. Mrs. Walsh, you're right. I didn't tell you the extent of what happened between Charles and myself. He had been paying me a lot of attention, and I liked it. He was charming and I was flattered. On a few occasions, Charles and I met at a restaurant under the guise of discussing the club fundraiser. It felt wrong but I was lonely. He showered me with kind words and flirted with me, just a little bit. Then one night, when he walked me to my car—" She paused as tears began to fall down her cheeks.

Donald's face softened as he looked at her. His anger dissipated as he wiped away her tears. "It's okay, Sharon, I'm here. Just tell them what happened."

"At the car, Charles grabbed my arm and made a pass at me," Sharon continued. "I drew back. I would never cheat on my husband. Charles's face changed. He looked brutish and cruel. He grabbed me by my hair and forced me to kiss him. Then he punched me in the head. He told me we were going to have a lot of fun together and walked away. I was hurt and frightened. I went home and told Donald what happened. The wallop Charles gave me on my head left a welt for a week. Donald was so understanding. He forgave my foolishness immediately and took care of me. From then on, I was scared of Charles. I avoided him as best I could but he continued to heckle me whenever he saw me. He seemed to enjoy the fear I had developed of him."

I nodded. "I suspected as much. In the last few days, I've heard other accounts of similar experiences. I figured you were probably no different. I'm sorry that happened to you."

"I didn't tell you because it was so humiliating. Donald has just been trying to protect me," she pleaded, looking from me to Detective Jones.

"Do you suspect your husband killed Charles?" I asked.

"No. No, he wouldn't," she pleaded.

"So why did you threaten to kill me, Sharon?" I asked.

Donald instantly lashed out viciously. "How dare you—" he began. But he stopped short of finishing his sentence as he glanced at his wife.

Sharon had turned white and looked scared. She was shaking like a leaf.

Donald's puffed up chest now deflated as he implored her, "Honey, you didn't—"

She hung her head and began to cry. "I'm sorry. I was scared. I thought you were going to blame Donald. I didn't know what to do."

"Lucky for you, it was messy and rushed," I said. "Completely opposite from the style of the real killer. That's what had been nagging me. The note didn't suit the crime. Simple."

"I was just trying to intimidate you. I didn't want you to find out—" She broke off, not able to finish her sentence.

"Find out what?" Donald demanded, "that *I* killed Charles? You thought I did it?" He dropped her hand and looked at her incredulously.

"I was too scared to ask," she admitted meekly.

"You made the investigation more confusing," Detective Jones rebuked her. "Luckily, Mrs. Walsh saw past your sloppy attempt to help your husband."

My heart went out to Sharon. "We know Donald didn't kill him," I informed her gently.

"The evidence just didn't quite add up," Detective Jones concurred.

A dramatic look of relief washed over Sharon's face. Donald's position once again softened, watching his wife struggle with emotion. A loving gaze was exchanged between the pair. I turned my focus toward William and Erica.

William looked around, panicked. "Why are you looking at me? I told you I didn't know Charles was planning to break up our partnership. I have no motive. He was a friend and associate for over twenty years. I had no knowledge of this violent, despicable behavior."

My gaze shifted to Erica and I met her expressionless eyes. "How about you, Erica? Were you aware of Charles's dark side?"

"Of course not. He kept it well hidden from everyone he cared about. How would I know?" she said.

"Only through experience," I said.

"That's ridiculous. I worked for Charles and William for years. He never hit on me. I never saw *any* sign. He had me fooled as much as anyone else."

"What about on Friday, Erica?" I asked.

"What about it? As I told you then, I knocked on the boathouse door and when Charles didn't answer I headed over to the house where I met you ladies," she said.

"You didn't try and convince him to remain partners with William?" I asked.

"I didn't see Charles that night. I also didn't know

about Charles leaving the firm. Even if I did, it wouldn't be my place to interfere."

"Not unless you were trying to help the man you love—" I suggested.

"Just who do you think you are?" William interrupted.

"Mr. Stormwell, please allow Erica to answer a few questions," Detective Jones requested firmly.

"I don't see how our relationship has any bearing on this case," William said, looking defensive.

"You will, Mr. Stormwell," I replied.

"Why should she be subjected to your nosy and inappropriate inquiry?" he demanded.

"Would you prefer I ask the questions?" Detective Jones asked. "We can do that. It'll just involve handcuffs, an interrogation room, and, to be perfectly honest, won't be nearly as friendly."

Erica squeezed his arm gently, "It's okay, Will. Let's just get this over with."

Mr. Stormwell reluctantly remained quiet, allowing me to continue. "Why have you kept your relationship private?"

"I didn't want to choose between love and a career. It would be unseemly for a partner's wife to work full-time at the office, so William and I decided not to marry and keep our relationship discreet, until now of course," she said with an edge.

"But Mary and Charles knew the extent of your relationship," I suggested.

"Of course," Erica replied curtly.

"Did you really go to bring Charles's clubs unannounced on Friday or did Charles call you first?" I asked.

"Why does it matter?" she said bitterly.

"It just struck me as odd that you'd go to Charles's private retreat uninvited, especially when you were expected at the main house," I remarked.

"Your point?" she asked.

"My guess is that Charles lured you to his boathouse under the pretense of needing his new golf clubs. Once there, I assume he attacked you and you reacted quicker and more effectively than he was prepared for, resulting in his death," I said, without judgement.

Erica didn't have a chance to reply before William grabbed her hand. "This is getting outright preposterous. I will no longer listen to this nonsense."

"Not before we take a look at your shoes, Miss Dorner," Detective Jones said.

"What do you want with my shoes?" Erica asked, looking stone-faced.

"I want to see if that stiletto heel matches the puncture wound in Charles Whitmore's chest," he answered.

Erica dropped William's hand. "Let me save you the trouble. It's a match," she confirmed.

William looked at Erica, shocked. "What do you mean?"

"What happened on Friday night, Erica?" I interrupted.

She paused and let out a big sigh. "You're theory is correct. He called me earlier on Friday from the club and asked me to bring the new golf set down to his boathouse later on. I was surprised, because when he left the office the day before, he walked right past them, commenting that he'd need to practice with them before bringing them on the course. However, I agreed and brought them, thinking it would be, as you guessed, a good opportunity to convince Charles not to part ways with William. I had found out the day before when I overheard Charles talking on the phone with one of his golf friends. I didn't want him to break up the firm. It would jeopardize William's career. But when I got there, Charles had been drinking heavily. I think he had forgotten that I was coming. At first, he seemed jumpy, almost embarrassed, and he apologized. He said he'd had a terrible argument with Mary. I brought up the subject of William, and he grew instantly agitated. I started to become uncomfortable and his demeanor became more bizarre and aggressive. He took out a bottle of wine and a few glasses from a cupboard and offered me a drink. I declined and he almost snarled at me. I had never seen Charles like that before."

Mary sighed. "I'm so sorry, Erica. That must've been an awful shock."

She nodded, "It was quite a surprise. He had always treated me very respectfully. But that night he was like a different person. He laughed when I tried to bring up William again. He started on a tirade about how women were trying to overstep their place, trying to take away power from men. It wasn't making sense. Then he hit on me. I was caught off guard and backed away. Without a word, he then punched me in the head so hard that my ears rang. I looked him in the eye. With a wicked grin on his face, he asked me if I wanted to play. I started to shake. He came at me again. My instincts took over. I didn't know what he was planning, but I wasn't going to let him hurt me again. I looked for something to defend myself with. But he had me cornered. He hit me again on the head, and it knocked me over. In a panic, I grabbed my shoe.

"I only wanted to keep him away. The next time he came at me, I swung my shoe toward him. He stumbled, falling backward, but he got up and had a menacing expression on his face. I knew then he wasn't going to stop. I was so frightened I took both hands together and swung again, plunging the heel toward his advancing figure with all my strength. This time I knew my swing connected. Charles fell backward again but this time he didn't get up. I pulled the heel out of his chest and blood started pouring out if his body. With that, I knew he was dead. A sense of calm washed over me. I guess my instincts took over. I cleaned my shoe and went to the house. I knew I just killed a man but the relief of having escaped that situation alive was all I could think about. I didn't think anybody would believe what really happened so I decided not to tell anyone."

The silence in the room was complete. Even William Stormwell had to take a minute to process Erica's story.

"You were so relaxed at the dinner, Erica. It doesn't make any sense," Mary said desperately.

"I think I was still in shock. It didn't really sink in until the next day. All I kept thinking was how lucky I was to be safe—that he could never hurt me again. Somehow, I separated my relief from the fact that I killed a man. I'm so sorry, Mar—"

"That animal deserved what he got. Don't apologize for that, Erica," William interrupted fiercely.

"Erica, William is right. You were only defending yourself," Mary said wistfully.

She stood tall. "I'm not sorry Charles is dead. But I *am* sorry for putting the people I care about through a terrible ordeal, especially you, Mary. I never would've let you go to prison for it."

"Where did you learn to defend yourself like that? I'm still lost," Donald interjected.

"I don't know. It was a gut reaction. It all just happened so quickly," Erica said throwing her arms up, as if at a loss.

"Well, you don't become a tennis champ without some outstanding skill and reflex," Mary attested.

"Mary, I hope you can learn to forgive me one day," Erica said.

Mary fumbled. "I need time to process all of this."

"I think we all do, Mary," Jo agreed.

"Miss Dorner, I need you to come with me. You are under arrest for the murder of Charles Whitmore," Detective Jones said.

"Of course," Erica said without argument.

"You will not go to prison for this, I'll see to it, Erica. I promise," William said desperately, "The best criminal lawyer I know will be at your side within the hour."

"Thank you, William," Erica said in almost a whisper. Detective Jones led her out in handcuffs without incident. William followed right behind.

As quickly as the scene unfolded, it dispersed as well. No one wanted to stick around and discuss what happened. All the guests were gone as soon as they could get out the door. It was not that people weren't curious about it. In fact, virtually everyone shot me a sideways glance before leaving Mary's. But I think the shock of what transpired sparked a reaction of fear and the desire to get away from the truth. It was just too much to handle all at once.

Within minutes, the only ones left standing in the room were Mary, Jo, Ava, and me. My friends were giving me pretty curious looks, too. But they were not as anxious to run. As if on cue, Mrs. Collins breezed into the sitting room and instructed us to move ourselves into the sunroom for coffee and tea. She had neatly prepared sandwiches and biscuits waiting for us.

"All right, you four. Sit down and relax. The drama is over for the day and it's time to unwind and discuss.

Grab a nibble with your beverage, if you please. I'll be in the kitchen if you need me." She looked at me and gave me a knowing wink. Obviously, she had overheard what happened.

I let out a big sigh and offered a weak smile in return, hoping she could read the thanks in my eyes.

"I need to freshen up," Mary said. "I'll join you in just a few minutes."

My heart went out to her, yet again. "Are you okay, Mary?"

"Let me quickly say this: I am, first and foremost, thankful for everything you three have done for me in the last week. You have proven I am innocent of a crime so I will not have to face life in prison and, on top of that, you found out who killed my husband."

Jo looked concerned. "You're not really answering the question."

"Everything will sort itself out. I will get past this and move on. Now, I need to go and have a hot shower and I will be back in fifteen minutes. We can talk about my fragile emotional state but not until I'm feeling a little more human. I think I still smell like a jail cell," she said in a weak attempt at humor.

"Of course, go on," Jo said, giving her a big hug.

Mary smiled sadly at us and left the room.

Jo watched her go. "That poor woman has been through so much in the last few days."

"She has," I agreed, "but you know as well as we do,

that Mary is a strong woman. She's going to be just fine. We'll be there to support her every step."

Ava grabbed a sandwich and sat down, "I need to change the subject for a minute. Can somebody explain to me what the Hell just happened?"

Jo looked at me and nodded adamantly. "Yes, Izzy, I have to second that sentiment. I'm completely lost as to when this whole mess got cleared up. I had thought we were starting to narrow in on Donald Wright as the prime suspect? When—What—" She apparently lost her train of thought, threw her arms up in the air, and looked around confused. Next, she grabbed a cookie and took a big bite as if in defeat.

I sat next to Jo. "I'm sorry for keeping you in the dark about Charles's murder. The truth is I only figured out what happened a few hours ago. The truth dawned on me in the library parking lot as I was looking at a French magazine that belonged to Sharon Wright. She was going to lend the magazine to me for Erica, who I guessed would love it since she is not only French, but also a very fashionable lady. That led me to consider how much ad-miration I felt for her—the successes she had already ex-perienced: her career, her worldliness, her sporting ac-complishments. She had so many strengths. But then that word: strength, lingered in my mind. I wasn't sure why. It all started to unravel from there: I realized she was one of the few women who would be physically capable of committing the murder. She also had the opportunity and the motive. Ava and I immediately drove to the police station once the truth had dawned on me. When I detailed what I believed had occurred the night Charles was killed, Detective Jones swore Ava and myself to absolute secrecy.

"You don't think I can keep a secret?" Jo asked, looking hurt.

"There really wasn't any time, besides, if we told you that Erica had plunged her stiletto into Charles's heart, would you really be able to act normal in front of her?" I challenged.

"Right, good point. Carry on," she said, accepting my description.

Ava winked at me. "You're a real detective now, Izzy."

Jo didn't look ready to put it away. "Why would Charles attack Erica now? They've worked together for years without incident. He had planned to lure her there even before he started drinking, using a request for the golf clubs as the excuse. He must've had something sinister planned, based on his pattern of abuse and sexual assault. That is still unclear to me."

"Revenge," I said.

"Revenge for what?" Ava asked.

I looked at Jo and Ava. "Charles never forgave William for pressuring him into choosing the law firm over his brother's wishes for him to join the navy together. He wanted to get him back in a way that would hurt William like he was hurt by the death of his beloved brother."

Ava looked confused. "I thought he was doing that by breaking up the law firm."

"That was just the beginning. But that alone wasn't personal enough for Charles. He wanted it to destroy William's life, his happiness," I suggested.

Ava twirled one of her silky dark curls around her finger. "What could hurt more than putting a man's career in jeopardy?"

Mary had rejoined us and had been quietly listening up until then. "Love," she said simply.

"That's right, Mary," I said, "What better way to hurt a man than seduce the woman he loved? My guess is that was the original plan, anyways. But after the fight with Mary, he probably had some drinks and forgot Erica was even coming. Then unable to control his drunken rage, his dark side came out and he attacked her. He didn't take into account Erica's exceptional power. It must've come as quite a shock to him."

"Talk about a killer serve," Ava stated with a shudder.

Jo slapped a hand over her mouth to cover up an inappropriate smile. "It looked like it was even a shock to William, who I didn't realize was her...special someone? How did I miss that?".

"They kept their relationship very private," Mary acknowledged. "How did you know, Izzy?"

"A few things gave it away. First of all, it was the car. I couldn't imagine that she could afford a flashy car with her salary," I said.

"You guys have almost the same car," Ava said.

"Yes, that's what made me think of it. The only reason *we* have it is because Frank rebuilt it after a customer brought it by the shop with serious damage. He bought it for next to nothing and made it a personal project. But it wasn't just the car. Erica knew personal and intimate information regarding the relationship between William and Charles. None of which would be in the office files."

Jo raised her hand. "So, did she want to frame William? Is that why she told you their history?"

I shook my head. "No, she was sure to give him an alibi at the time of Charles's death. Remember she asked Mrs. Collins to phone William when she first arrived? She claimed it was so he would know she would be late but I believe it was strictly to prove he was home when the murder took place. The phone call could then be validated by Mrs. Collins, thereby giving William an air tight alibi. She just wanted the police to see that Charles had enemies and a dark side to him. I believe she figured his death would remain a mystery."

"Brilliant," Ava said.

Jo cast her eyes down to the floor. "I wonder what's going to happen to her."

I rubbed my forehead. "Given the circumstances, I doubt the charge of murder will stick."

Mary attempted a smile. "Especially with the help of a good lawyer. Isn't that ironic?"

Ava matched her expression. "What do you make of all this, Mary?"

"I really don't know yet. I think I need to sleep for about a week and then try and piece it together. I honestly can't get my head around what's happened and the kind of man I was married to," she confessed.

I guessed her mind would still be spinning from the events of the last week. "Try and focus on the sleep and as little else as you can. Until you've recovered yourself, nothing is going to make sense."

She put one hand over her mouth momentarily. "If it ever will."

Jo reached over and rubbed her back. "It will, Mary. I promise."

Ava and I then left to go home. Jo still had the rest of the week to stay at Mary's and we agreed to get back together in a few days.

I was always happy to go home after being away, but I couldn't remember a time I had such a sense of relief, as well. It felt like the last few days were catching up with me as I was pulling into the driveway. Frank must've heard the car because he opened the front door as I approached it.

He had a blanket waiting on the couch and a big glass of water next to it. I curled up on the couch and Frank sat next to me. I filled him in on the last day's events, and he listened quietly, interrupting me only to clarify a few times that he understood the bizarre truth I was telling him.

Over the next few days, things quickly went back to normal, and I had to remind myself that Charles's murder and the fallout of events afterward were not a dream.

Thursday afternoon, Ava called me and asked me if I had spoken to Jo or Mary. I hadn't. We agreed that I would pick her up after dinner and head over to Mary's. I wondered how Mary was coping with the reality of what happened.

I pulled up to Ava's, and she practically bounded out of the house. The scene was eerily similar to when I picked her up less than a week before.

I grinned. "Hey there, Miss Energy."

She hopped in the car like a ball of fire. "Hello, my dear. I'm feeling confident our comrades are doing well. I'm very happy we're getting together again so soon."

"Do they know we're coming?"

"No, but I'm sure they'll be there and happy to see us," she said.

My nerves were hopping around my stomach. "I hope so."

She rested her chin on her fist and examined me while I drove. "Now listen, Izzy, just because you have an apparent knack for solving murders, doesn't mean you'll be blamed for the crime."

"I just wish it had turned out differently."

"Differently, how? Have Mary still be in jail? Have the murder still unsolved? You did everyone a great service by figuring out what happened. In truth, I'm still a little amazed at your new found skills."

"I had the best partners an amateur detective could

ask for. And I think lady luck was on our side," I said truthfully.

"I'm not going to argue. Let's not do it again any time soon though, okay?"

"It's a deal," I agreed.

When we pulled up to Mary's, we could see two lounge chairs overlooking the ocean with what could only be our friends stretched out on them. It was a sight I was happy to see.

Ava smiled at me knowingly. "I told you they'd be faring all right."

I looked at her and nodded in hopeful anticipation. We walked toward them and Ava shouted ahead, as she recognized that sneaking up behind them, no matter how unintentional, would not be a good way to say hello under the circumstances. "Any more chairs in the vicinity to add to the party?"

Mary and Jo popped their heads up and both gave a big wave.

Mary was smiling from ear to ear. She gave us each a big hug. "We were wondering when you two would grace us with your presence."

Ava stood back and assessed Mary. "You, my dear, are looking about a thousand times better."

"Ava's right," I said, "It's wonderful to see you looking like yourself again."

"Well, thank you two. I'm feeling even better, I am happy to confess."

I felt my nerves carried away with the ocean breeze. "I can't tell you what a relief that is."

She tipped her head toward me. "Thanks to you, all I have to worry about at this point is mourning a despicable husband, and to making peace with a particularly bizarre week."

Ava let out a hoot. "Amen to that."

"Looking at what I could have been facing as an alternative," Mary continued. "I consider myself getting off easy." She paused. "And Jo has been incredibly doting and kind since this whole mess has ended, which has made it so much easier to deal with."

Jo smiled affectionately at Mary.

"I'm just glad the truth came out." I said.

"I think we all are," Jo agreed.

Mrs. Collins appeared, awkwardly trying to carry two more lounge chairs from the side yard. Ava and I went to assist her. She was quite out of breath by the time we reached her.

"Thank you for your help, ladies," she puffed. "And I'm not so much referring to the chairs, if you get my meaning."

"Right back at you, Mrs. C.," Ava said, giving Mrs. Collins a big smile before the doting housekeeper marched back inside.

We brought our chairs back to where our friends were sitting. We set them up and collapsed into them as the sun emerged from behind some clouds.

"Can I ask a favor?" Mary asked from her idle seat.

I answered first. "Of course, Mary, anything."

"Can we talk about something normal? I'd like to have a regular conversation for a change."

"Understood," Jo said.

Mary pointed her arm straight up in the air. "I have one more request."

I was the first one to reply, again. "What is it, Mary?"

"Can we go somewhere else next year for our girls' weekend?"

I threw both hands up in the air and shook my fists. "Wouldn't have it any other way."

Ava and Jo modeled the weird hand gestures in support of the idea. We all broke out into an inexplicable giggle.

Although things would never be quite the same, I knew we were going to get through the tragedy of events together. Mary would be all right and the rest of us would be there to support her when she wasn't. I felt a smile creep onto my face that felt damn good.

About the Author

Lynn McPherson grew up in various parts of Canada, from the Canadian Rockies to the big city of Toronto. Travel was always a part of her life, starting with a trip to Europe at the curious age of two. Many moons later, Lynn's love of adventure and exploration never ceased, eventually leading her to the exciting world of writing, where she is free to go anywhere, anytime. Having a particular love of New England, possibly stemming from a snowy winter's night spent at a cozy inn, Lynn has always known this is where her mystery series must take place. She is a member of the *International Thriller Writers* and *Sisters in Crime*.

CPSIA information can be obtained
at www.ICGtesting.com
Printed in the USA
LVOW10s1724200917
549415LV00013B/1112/P